"I love you, Celia. Marry me."

With happiness coursing through her, Celia sat up and stared at him. "You're serious?"

"I've never been more serious in my life."

Cameron's response stunned her into silence. She wanted nothing more than to remain on Solitaire with him, but she wondered why he'd undergone yet another change of heart.

He grasped her shoulders, then slid his hands down the length of her arms. She responded to his touch with a shiver of pleasure, an echo of what they'd just shared.

"If you remain on Solitaire," he said, "it must be because you love me. I couldn't bear having you here if you didn't return my love."

She lifted her lips to his once more, then after a long moment pulled away. "I do love you, Cameron, and I will marry you."

He pulled her down beside him, sculpting his body to hers like nesting spoons. "Sleep well, Celia. We have much to do tomorrow."

In the warm shelter of his arms she fell instantly asleep.

Had she known what the future held for her, she wouldn't have slept at all.

Dear Harlequin Intrigue Reader,

Deck the halls with romance and suspense as we bring you four new stories that will wrap you up tighter than a present under your Christmas tree!

First we begin with the continuing series by Rita Herron, NIGHTHAWK ISLAND, where medical experiments on an island off the coast of Georgia lead to some dangerous results. Cole Hunter does not know who he is, and the only memories he has are of Megan Wells's dead husband. And why does he have these intimate *Memories of Megan*?

Next, Susan Kearney finishes her trilogy THE CROWN AFFAIR, which features the Zared royalty and the treachery they must confront in order to save their homeland. In book three, a prickly, pretty P.I. must pose as a prince's wife in order to help his majesty uncover a deadly plot. However, will she be able to elude his *Royal Pursuit* of her heart?

In Charlotte Douglas's *The Bride's Rescuer*, a recluse saves a woman who washes up on his lonely island, clothed only in a tattered wedding dress. Cameron Alexander hasn't seen a woman in over six years, and Celia Stevens is definitely a woman, with secrets of her own. But whose secrets are more deadly? And also join Jean Barrett for another tale with the Hawke Family Detective Agency in the Christmastime cross-country journey titled *Official Escort*.

Best wishes to all of our loyal readers for a "breathtaking" holiday season!

Sincerely,

Denise O'Sullivan
Associate Senior Editor
Harlequin Intrigue

THE BRIDE'S RESCUER

CHARLOTTE DOUGLAS

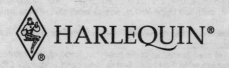

TORONTO • NEW YORK • LONDON
AMSTERDAM • PARIS • SYDNEY • HAMBURG
STOCKHOLM • ATHENS • TOKYO • MILAN • MADRID
PRAGUE • WARSAW • BUDAPEST • AUCKLAND

ISBN 0-373-22691-8

THE BRIDE'S RESCUER

Copyright © 2002 by Charlotte H. Douglas

This edition published by arrangement with Harlequin Books S.A.

® and TM are trademarks of the publisher. Trademarks indicated with
® are registered in the United States Patent and Trademark Office, the
Canadian Trade Marks Office and in other countries.

Visit us at www.eHarlequin.com

Printed in U.S.A.

Charlotte Douglas has loved a good story since she learned to read at the age of three. After years of teaching that love of books to her students, she now enjoys creating stories of her own. Often her books are set in one of her three favorite places: Montana, where she and her husband spent their honeymoon; the mountains of North Carolina, where they're building a summer home; or Florida, near the Gulf of Mexico on Florida's west coast, where she's lived most of her life.

Books by Charlotte Douglas

HARLEQUIN INTRIGUE
380—DREAM MAKER
434—BEN'S WIFE
482—FIRST-CLASS FATHER
515—A WOMAN OF MYSTERY
536—UNDERCOVER DAD
611—STRANGER IN HIS ARMS*
638—LICENSED TO MARRY
668—MONTANA SECRETS
691—THE BRIDE'S RESCUER

HARLEQUIN AMERICAN ROMANCE
591—IT'S ABOUT TIME
623—BRINGING UP BABY
868—MONTANA MAIL-ORDER WIFE*

*Identity Swap

Don't miss any of our special offers. Write to us at the following address for information on our newest releases.

Harlequin Reader Service
U.S.: 3010 Walden Ave., P.O. Box 1325, Buffalo, NY 14269
Canadian: P.O. Box 609, Fort Erie, Ont. L2A 5X3

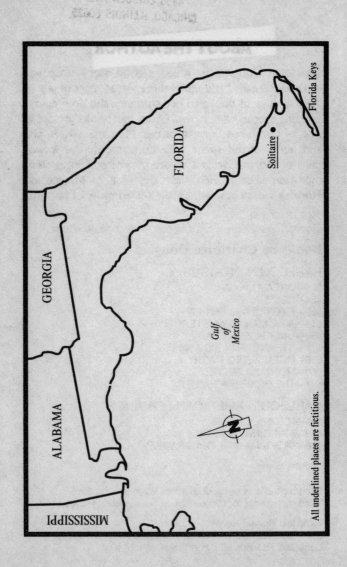

MISSISSIPPI

ALABAMA

GEORGIA

FLORIDA

Solitaire •

Florida Keys

Gulf
of
Mexico

All underlined places are fictitious.

CAST OF CHARACTERS

Cameron Alexander—A compellingly handsome and enigmatic British exile, the owner of Solitaire Island.

Celia Stevens—Flees from marriage with one dangerous man only to end up in potentially greater peril.

Mrs. Givens—Cameron's devoted housekeeper, who has raised him from an infant.

Noah—Cameron's handyman, another exile with secrets of his own.

Darren Walker—Celia's fiancé with a deadly past.

Jack Utley—A hired killer.

Prologue

Celia Stevens stood before the cheval mirror in the bride's parlor of the Chapel by the Sea, smoothing the satin skirt of her Vera Wang gown and adjusting her flowing veil with a trembling hand.

She'd bought the dress on impulse, the first one she'd tried on. But that whim had turned out okay, she assured herself. She'd purchased her bookstore, Sand Castles, on impulse too, and the business was headed for success. Another impulse had compelled her to agree with Darren, her fiancé, to move up the date of their wedding to October, not waiting for the June ceremony she'd always dreamed of. She'd been spontaneous all her life, rushing headlong into one experience after another, and so far everything had turned out fine.

So why was she feeling today as if her luck was about to run out?

"Are you okay?" Tracey Morris, her best friend and maid of honor, hovered behind her, and Celia could read the concern in Tracey's brown eyes in the reflecting glass.

"Sure," Celia said with a bravado she didn't feel. She couldn't meet her own gaze in the mirror. The trepidations she was experiencing were the normal prewedding jitters, that's all. "It's my wedding day. The happiest day of my life."

"Is it?"

Celia whirled and faced her friend. "Of course."

She didn't sound convincing, even to herself, and she could tell Tracey wasn't buying her declaration. "I'm marrying a man who loves me, who's thoughtful, kind—"

"Who gives you goose bumps and makes you hear bells ring and see fireworks when he walks into a room?" Tracey prodded.

"That's the stuff of fairy tales," Celia insisted. "We're mature adults—"

"Hogwash," Tracey muttered loudly. "This is marriage we're talking about, not a business contract. Do you love him, Cel?"

"There're all kinds of love. I care about Darren. Just not in the Hollywood head-over-heels fashion you seem to think so important."

Celia sank into the nearest chair, heedless of wrinkling the bridal satin. She'd had this same conversation with Tracey many times before, and each time she'd begged her friend not to broach the subject again. She couldn't blame Tracey, however, for her skepticism. Celia had misgivings of her own. Ever since her parents had died in that horrendous car crash, she'd been alone. When Darren Walker had entered her life and offered marriage and a family,

Celia, sick and tired of solitude, had leaped at his proposal. A home, a husband, and the prospect of children promised to fill the void left by her parents' deaths.

Now that the hour of her wedding was almost upon her, however, her confidence that she'd made the right decision was wavering. Tracey's probing questions only fed Celia's uncertainty. But she'd come too far to back out now. The wedding gifts had been opened, the church was filled with relatives and friends, the yacht club decorated for the reception, and in just ten minutes, Darren would be waiting for her at the altar.

"You've always been my best friend." With a rueful smile, Tracey shook her head and held out the skirt of her gown. "For no one else would I wear this bilious shade of pink." Her expression sobered. "But I think you're making a terrible mistake. It's not too late to call it off."

For an instant, Celia almost agreed, but Darren was such a sweet man, she couldn't desert him. She wouldn't leave him standing at the altar like some pathetic character in a television sitcom.

"I'm marrying Darren," she declared, as much to shore up her own courage as to assure Tracey.

With a resigned shake of her head, Tracey headed toward the door. "Our bouquets are in the refrigerator in the church kitchen. When I bring them back, it's show time."

Her friend slipped out the door, and Celia clasped her hands in her lap to cease their trembling. Was she doing the right thing? She'd had niggling doubts from the day she'd accepted Darren's proposal, but she'd always managed to shove them aside by considering the positive aspects of marriage to him. He was handsome, wealthy, well-mannered, well-educated...she ran through his attributes like a mantra, hoping to staunch the panic welling within her.

With a start, she realized she was no longer alone in the room. A middle-aged woman with elegantly coifed graying hair stood just inside the parlor door. From the cut of her designer suit and the jewels on her fingers, Celia guessed her to be one of Darren's guests.

Celia rose to her feet. "If you're looking for the sanctuary—"

"I'm looking for you," the woman said. "You *are* Celia Stevens, aren't you?"

Celia nodded. "Who are you?"

"My name's not important. Time is running out. You can't marry that man."

"Darren?"

The woman grimaced. "Is that what he's calling himself these days?"

"What do you mean?"

The woman moved closer. "When he married my daughter, his name was David Weller."

Celia felt as if she'd entered a twilight zone. The woman seemed too self-possessed, too rational to be crazy. "Darren's never been married."

At least that's what he'd told her, and he'd never given her reason to doubt him. Or had he?

Celia's thoughts whirled in confusion.

The woman nodded grimly. "Of course, that's what he told you." She slipped an expensive handbag from beneath her arm, opened it, and extracted a newspaper clipping. "See for yourself."

Celia took the paper from the woman and walked toward the window. The late afternoon sunlight fell on the newsprint, a photograph of a bride and groom with the heading, "Seffner-Weller Wedding." The groom staring back at her was Darren Walker. Or his double.

"There must be some mistake," Celia said, feeling as if the floor had dropped out from under her.

"There is," the woman insisted, "and you're making it."

Confused, Celia shook her head and sagged onto the sofa. "This can't be Darren."

"It is. I watched him entering the pastor's study. It's the same man, all right."

"Why did your daughter divorce him?"

"She didn't."

Celia's eyes widened and her stomach lurched. "You mean Darren is still married?"

Terrible pain and sudden tears filled the woman's eyes. "He's a widower."

Relief flooded through her. At least Darren wasn't a bigamist. "I'm sorry."

"Not as sorry as you'll be if you go through with this. He *murdered* my daughter."

Her nausea returned, and Celia rubbed her eyes with her fists. "You must be mistaken. If he's a murderer, he'd be in jail."

"He's a clever murderer, and an even better con man."

"Look, Mrs. Seffner, I'm sorry for your loss, but—"

"Listen to me, girl. If my own daughter had listened, she'd still be alive today. Did you sign a prenuptial agreement?"

Celia shook her head. "It seemed pointless. Darren has more money than I—"

"My daughter's money, left to her by her paternal grandfather. David—Darren refused to sign the agreement I insisted upon, and my poor daughter was too besotted to care. Just weeks after the wedding, she died in a boating accident on the lake near their home. David found her. Her death was suspicious, but no one's been able to prove he did it—yet."

"How long has it been?"

"Six months. David disappeared after the funeral. I've been searching for him ever since."

Celia reeled with shock. Darren had entered her life only five months ago, just a short time after her parents' death. She had thought his willingness to help settle her parents' affairs had been kindness, but in looking back, she recognized his intense interest in their estate.

And her inheritance.

The newspaper clipping was testament to his untruthfulness. Why hadn't he told her of his previous marriage? What else hadn't he told her?

The woman stepped forward and tipped Celia's chin until their eyes met. "I know your mother's

gone, so I'm begging you in her name, don't go
through with this wedding. Take time to investigate
what I've told you.''

She smoothed a strand of hair from Celia's face in
a gesture that reminded her so much of her own
mother, she had to fight back tears. The stranger then
pivoted on her expensive high heels and left the room.

In the solitude, Celia's doubts swelled and multi-
plied. Snippets of formerly harmless conversations
with Darren replayed in her memory, laden now with
sinister implications. He had no family, he'd told her.
And he'd been vague about his work. Investments,
he'd called it. Nothing exciting. Nothing she'd want
to hear about. He'd traveled in his work, never really
settling down, so there was no place he called home.
And most of his close friends and business associates
were traveling out of the country and would be unable
to attend the wedding. She had swallowed his explanations and excuses whole, never dreaming they
might not be the truth.

Suddenly, she felt as if she couldn't breathe. She
hurried to the parlor door and into the corridor. Running as if the devil himself were after her, bridal gown
lifted to her knees and her veil trailing in the wind,
she raced from the church, sprinted through the filled
parking lot, and dodged traffic as she crossed the main
road that bisected the beach community. Avoiding the
clubhouse at the yacht club, she followed the pathway
to the marina at its rear and thundered down the dock
toward the farthest slip.

Her father's sailboat, a classic 32-foot Morgan, was

moored in its usual spot. With shaking hands, Celia disengaged the lines, tossed them onboard, and leaped onto the deck. Within minutes, she had the auxiliary engines started and was moving the boat into the channel.

Suddenly the voice of the harbormaster, a man she'd known since she was a child, sounded over the public address system. "Celia, return to port. There's a storm brewing."

She'd weathered storms in the Morgan before. Returning to port meant facing Darren, a man with possible homicidal tendencies, and over fifty curious wedding guests. Returning also meant dealing with the ominous accusations of the strange woman, Mrs. Seffner. And worst of all, returning meant admitting to herself that she'd almost married a man she didn't love.

A storm, the harbormaster had warned. Maybe that was just what she needed. A big wind to blow all her troubles away.

As soon as Celia reached the channel, she raised the sails and headed west into the Gulf of Mexico and the gathering storm.

Chapter One

"Is she dead?"

The deep drawling voice invaded Celia's consciousness, and *dead* ricocheted in her mind like a frightened bird in a too-small cage. She couldn't be dead. A dead person felt nothing. Her ribs ached. Her head pounded. Her arms and legs throbbed. Her skin burned from the scorching sun, but she shivered in the cool breeze.

The coolness of a shadow fell across her, blocking the sun's assault, and strong, gentle fingers probing her neck for a pulse pressed her cheek deeper into hot sand. She winced as breaking waves of saltwater stung her lacerated ankles.

All around her a peculiar blackness vibrated with shifting lights, shapeless moats of brightness and color that ebbed and flowed like the water at her feet. Weariness seeped through her, making her eyelids too heavy to open. She wanted to cover her ears to block the relentless roar of the surf, but her hands refused to respond. Exhausted, she settled deeper into the soft, hot sand and drifted back into darkness.

"You gonna have to pry her hands off that board." The voice roused her once more, and awe tinged the words, uttered in a thick and lazy Southern drawl. "Hanging on to it's probably the only thing saved her."

"Dear God, why did you send her here?" A second deep, rich voice, this one with a cultured British accent, rang with torment, and gentle fingers traced the curve of her jaw and cupped her face. "Careful with her hands, Noah."

Someone loosened her fingers from an object she hadn't known they clasped, and she cried out in pain. The second man wrapped her in a garment—his shirt?—and her shivering eased. Strong arms lifted her from the sand and cradled her against a warm, hard body. The heat from his skin warmed her, and her shivering ceased.

"Rest easy, miss. We'll take good care of you."

The tenderness in the masculine British voice soothed her more than his words. The comforting rhythm of his heartbeats thudded where her cheek rested on his bare chest, and she relaxed in his embrace and opened her eyes. She focused slowly on a strong, tanned jaw, generous mouth, classic nose and wide amber eyes combined in a face so handsome it took her breath away.

Her sudden intake of air drew his attention, and her rescuer glanced down at her. His remarkable tawny eyes filled with tenderness.

Before she could ask his name, he called to the other man, the one he'd called Noah.

"I'm taking her to Mrs. Givens," the Englishman stated. "She'll care for her, but I want this woman kept out of my sight. Lock her in her room if she has to."

Celia struggled to reconcile the strangeness of his words with the tenderness she had seen in his expression. Maybe a blow to the head had addled her brains. Why would he want her locked away? She was in no shape to be a threat to anyone.

"You gonna be fine, miss." A wide smile broke across the ebony face of the man who walked beside them. Cool currents of air wafted across her sunburned skin, and the gently rocking motion of the Englishman's gait as he carried her from the beach lulled her back into unconsciousness.

CELIA SURFACED SLOWLY from the depths of darkness and glanced around her. She lay in a soft bed, alone in a strange room. Her fingers skimmed smooth, fresh sheets that smelled of lemons and sunshine. Above arched a high ceiling with open beams, and beyond the foot of the bed, French doors opened onto a covered veranda.

A warm breeze laden with the pungent tang of saltwater wafted through the sparsely furnished room and rippled white muslin curtains tied back from the doors. Another fragrance moved on the air, the heavy scent of oleander from the branches in a cloisonné vase on the dresser. The uneasy quiet, like a palpable presence, gathered in the room, hovering and threatening in the dim twilight.

What had her impulsiveness landed her in this time? She'd run away from her marriage, wrecked her boat in a storm, and ended up in a place she couldn't identify. Couldn't she do anything right?

The sounds of footsteps and swishing skirts broke the eerie stillness, the feeling of an intangible threat retreated, and the door beside her bed opened. A short, stout woman with gray curls, wearing a lavender cotton dress covered by a white apron, bustled into the room with a tray of food. She smiled, and lights danced in her deep green eyes.

"Ah, feeling better, are we? I'm Mrs. Givens, the housekeeper. Let me help you up."

Mrs. Givens slipped a plump arm beneath Celia's shoulders and braced extra pillows behind her.

"Where am I?" Celia asked in confusion.

"On an island, m'dear, off the southwest Florida coast."

"My boat?"

"You've been shipwrecked. We found you only half alive on the beach among the wreckage."

Dark, savage recollections of a terrible storm converged upon Celia, filling her with an unfamiliar dread. She closed her mind against the memories, too frightened to confront them. "What day is this?"

"Out here away from everything, I lose track of time." Mrs. Givens scrunched her pleasant features into a thoughtful grimace and counted on her fingers. "Today's Monday."

Monday.

Two days since the violent storm had broken her

sailboat into pieces, pitching her into a horrifying maelstrom of green water and sickly swirling clouds. She tossed the bedcovers back and swung her legs over the side. Someone had removed her clothes and dressed her in a white granny gown. Had it been the handsome Englishman or Mrs. Givens? Celia felt strangely vulnerable without her own garments. "Where are my clothes?"

"The storm ripped them to shreds." Mrs. Givens tapped a plump finger against her lips. "From what little was left, it looked like a wedding gown."

Celia ignored the curiosity in the woman's voice. After coming so close to dying, she wanted to appreciate being alive. She didn't want to think about weddings or Darren Walker. Not yet. "I'm Celia Stevens."

She had survived the shipwreck, and now she was alone, God knew where, among strangers. She had to get home. Her friends would be worried about her, especially after she'd run away from her wedding at the eleventh hour. But she couldn't travel in a granny gown.

"Could you lend me some clothes? Then maybe one of the men who found me could take me to the mainland."

Mrs. Givens sputtered in her haste to reply. "Good heavens, no! The nearest town is Key West."

Key West.

The words left her breathless. Somehow the storm had flung her hundreds of miles south in the Gulf. Now she faced a long drive home in a rental car. At least the trip would give her time to think of how to deal with the catastrophe she'd left behind her. "Key West will do fine."

"Mr. Alexander—"

"The Englishman?" The handsome but enigmatic man who'd ordered her locked in her room?

Mrs. Givens nodded. "Cameron Alexander hasn't been to Key West in over six years. He'll not be going there now."

"Why not?"

The housekeeper turned away, staring out through the veranda doors toward the Gulf of Mexico where the last rays of the setting sun shone. When she finally spoke, her voice sounded flat, emotionless. "You might say he's ill."

Strange. He hadn't looked ill—virile, attractive, and uncomfortable at the sight of an unexpected visitor, but not ill. He'd seemed extraordinarily kind—until his comment about locking her in her room. "What about the other man—the African-American? Can he take me?"

"Noah? Impossible."

"Why?" Impatience welled within her. She had to get home. She'd made her decision not to marry Darren, but in the process, she'd also made a mess of things. She had presents to return, letters of apology to write, and an inquiry to the police about the true identity of Darren Walker.

"Time enough to worry about such things later," Mrs. Givens said. "You just finish your supper. You have everything here you require, so there's no need for you to leave this room. I'll bring your breakfast in the morning.''

Mrs. Givens's reluctance to discuss her plight not only annoyed Celia, it alarmed her. The little woman seemed to be hiding something. Even so, Celia wished the woman would stay. Her company might keep the shadows and loneliness at bay.

''Mr. Alexander's room,'' the housekeeper said, ''is next to yours, but he prefers *not* to be disturbed. Rest well, and don't worry. You're perfectly safe here.''

Her instructions to remain in the room had been so pointed, Celia expected to be locked in, but when she tried the door to the hall after Mrs. Givens left, it opened freely.

Frustration had robbed her of her appetite, and she ignored the supper tray the housekeeper had left on the dresser. She would wait until everyone was asleep, then search for a telephone.

The darkness gathered with irritating slowness. Feeling hemmed in, almost a prisoner, she crossed the room onto the veranda, where broad fronds of cabbage palms crackled like stiff paper against the weathered, second-story balustrade. Beyond the house, a narrow path wound through a sea grape hedge toward dunes fringed with sea oats. Moonlight cut a silver swath across calm gulf waters. Directly below, a rectangle of light from a downstairs window fell on the ground. Abruptly the light disappeared. Mrs. Givens must have gone to bed.

The silence of the room oppressed Celia. The oil

lamp on the dresser indicated the house lacked electricity. She could do without power. What she needed was a telephone. Or maybe a generator and a short-wave radio. She'd search the house for a way to contact the mainland, to rent a boat, if necessary. A charter would be the quickest way to return to home and to work. And attending to her bookstore and its clients would be the best way to put her disastrous engagement behind her.

She doused the light on the dresser, crossed to the door, and laid her ear against the smooth pine panel. When she heard nothing, she opened the door and eased herself into the hallway.

Her bare feet made no sound on the stairs that descended to the lower hallway. Her head still throbbed, and vertigo made her unsteady, but she was determined to find a way to call for help.

In the dimness of the moonlight, the first room on the right appeared to be a study where the faint odor of leather, saddle soap and pipe tobacco hung in the air. In the darkness, she fumbled across the surface of the large desk, then searched the bookshelves, but she found nothing except books, papers and a humidor.

Celia returned to the hallway. Behind the door to the next room, Mrs. Givens's loud snores rattled. Celia tiptoed through the outer doors across a dogtrot to the kitchen. A massive woodstove, where embers lay banked for the night, dominated the room. Celia shook her head in sympathy. Without electricity and the convenience of modern appliances, the house-keeper had her work cut out for her.

Celia sneaked back into the main house and peered into the dining room, filled with the wicker and rattan furniture she'd expected in a Florida island house. But so far, no sign of a phone or any other means of communication.

Only one room remained, and her hopes of finding a means to call for help dwindled. She was treading softly toward the front room when dizziness engulfed her. She steadied herself against the paneling of the hallway, but her legs weakened, and for a moment, she feared she would faint. Her head throbbed from the blow she'd received when she capsized. Common sense told her to return to bed, but the need to find a radio or a phone kept her searching.

The door of the front room stood slightly ajar, and inside, a lamp burned low on the mantelpiece, illu-minating a life-sized portrait of a woman and boy. The woman, elegantly beautiful in a long formal gown, stood with her hand on the shoulder of a small boy with plump, rosy cheeks and a mischievous smile. The warm light and friendly expression of the child beckoned, and Celia entered the room.

A camel-backed sofa, flanked by deep chairs, faced the fireplace, whose black, gaping maw devoured a profusion of potted ferns and bromeliads. She shud-dered at the image and stepped around the sofa for a better look at the portrait, wondering if the pair were related to the present occupants.

Someone muttered incoherently behind her. Startled, she jumped and clasped her chest to prevent her heart from pounding through her breastbone. Whirling around, she discovered a man stretched out asleep upon the sofa. Her fear turned to surprise when she recognized Cameron Alexander, and surprise dissolved into a surge of relief. She would shake him awake and beg him to take her to the mainland.

But her vision blurred, her head throbbed, and the pain and dizziness returned. She slid weakly onto a chair beside the sofa. When the vertigo passed, she focused slowly on the man before her. With sunburnished hair the color of a lion's mane, he lay on his back. His unbuttoned shirt fell open, revealing the tanned muscles of a powerful chest, rising and falling in a hypnotic rhythm.

The strong lines of his sun-bronzed face, handsome, square-jawed and high-cheekboned, were softened by a lock of hair that fell over his forehead. A frown drew down the corners of his wide mouth, and a deep vertical line creased his forehead between his eyebrows, as if he dreamed unpleasant dreams.

His fitted pants accentuated muscular thighs, and his boots seemed more suitable for riding than boating. He had flung one arm over his head, and the other hung to the floor, where an empty brandy snifter rested in his curled fingers.

He didn't dress like a boater, no jeans or shorts or T-shirt, but, living on the island, he *had* to have a boat.

She rose, gripped the firm muscles of his shoulder, and shook him gently.

Instantly, his hand flew up and seized her wrist. In the same moment, his lids sprang open, and his eyes gleamed golden and wild. The dreaming frown intensified, and he stared at her so fiercely, she shivered in the warm air.

"What are you doing here?" His voice rumbled like distant thunder.

She pried his fingers from her wrist, realizing she couldn't have freed herself if he hadn't allowed it, and took a step back. "Looking for a way to contact the mainland to charter a boat. Do you have a radio?"

"No." In contrast to his harsh tone, his eyes flickered with sympathy.

"Can you take me to the mainland?"

"The closest town is Key West." He snarled the words, but his hands clenched and unclenched as if he fought some inner battle.

Instinctively, she retreated a few steps. "Will you take me there?"

He shook his head, as if to clear the sympathetic look from his eyes. "I haven't been to Key West in six years."

"But you said Key West is the closest town—"

"It is."

His gaze shifted past her to the portrait above the mantel, and when he spoke again, he seemed to be speaking to himself. "I haven't set foot there in six years and I have no intention of returning now."

Giddiness struck her once more, and she comprehended his words with difficulty.

"I have to go home—" The pain in her head

stabbed and swelled, the room spun wildly, her knees buckled, and the floor came up to meet her.

CAMERON ALEXANDER scooped the slender figure into his arms for the second time that day and placed her on the sofa. He had sworn to avoid her, to closet himself away until she left the island, but she'd found him.

He should awaken Mrs. Givens and leave the girl to her, but his resolve to keep away weakened as he feasted on the sight of her. His hands tingled with longing to bury themselves in the halo of her auburn hair with its highlights bleached by the sun. Golden lashes brushed her cheeks, hiding her sea-blue eyes, but the wide-eyed stare she had bestowed on him when he first gathered her off the beach remained etched in his mind.

He had seen no woman other than Mrs. Givens in over six years, but if he saw hundreds a day, the one before him would still captivate him. Fleetingly, he wished he'd met her years ago in the drawing room of a respectable London home, before his marriage, before his trouble. He'd believed he'd lost everything before he came to the island, but he hadn't calculated losing someone he had yet to meet. He'd had no way to predict a storm would wash such a woman onto his beach.

Poised and elegant, even in distress, yet poignantly vulnerable, Celia Stevens called forth all his protective instincts. A groan escaped his lips. He yearned to safeguard her, yet the most prudent thing he could do was place as much distance between himself and the woman before him as possible.

Had the Devil sent this vision to torment him? Worse yet, had God Almighty sent her as punishment for his grievous sins, a sight to conjure up memories of the horror he had spent so many years trying to forget?

He could not break his exile to take her away. He must avoid her, so there would never be another disaster.

Another death.

But even as he pledged to stay away, he could not refrain from staring at his gift from the sea.

CELIA OPENED HER EYES and gazed at the strange, lamplit ceiling in confusion. A glass clinked, and she looked toward the sideboard where the handsome stranger stood, filling a snifter with brandy from a crystal decanter.

"Feeling better?" The soft glow from the lamp bathed Cameron's face in golden light, and a concerned look replaced his earlier fierce expression.

She pulled herself up to a sitting position and curled into the corner of the sofa with her knees tucked beneath her, uncomfortably aware she wore only a thin cotton nightgown.

He handed her a snifter of brandy, folded his tall frame onto a chair beside her, raised his glass in a salute, and downed his drink in a great gulp. "Drink, Miss Stevens. The brandy will revive you, bring the color back to your cheeks."

She sipped the smooth cognac, and a flash of heat seared down her throat. "I've never been this giddy. When my boat broke up at sea, I banged my head somehow."

He leaned toward her and parted her hair with gentle fingers. "You have an angry knot there, but the skin isn't broken. Your dizziness should soon pass."

He smoothed her hair back with the palm of his hand in a gesture both comforting and disturbing.

"You never answered my question." Her throat burned from the brandy, and her voice came out a whisper.

"What question?" The edge returned to his tone, and his strange-colored eyes drilled into hers.

"Will you take me to Key West—or at least to the mainland?"

A wariness touched his eyes, and he appeared to withdraw inward. "No, I cannot."

"Can't or won't?"

As her strength returned, her anger grew. If he was the man of leisure he appeared, why couldn't he take a few hours to sail her to the mainland?

"Captain Biggins brings supplies to the island." He leaned back in his chair and rolled his glass between the palms of his strong, square hands. "He was here only a few days ago, but he will return in twelve weeks."

Dizziness and brandy made concentration difficult. "What's Captain Biggins got to do with me?"

Cameron refused to meet her eyes. "He will be

happy to take you to Key West, and I will gladly pay
your passage.''

''But twelve weeks—that's three months! I can't
stay here that long. I have a business to run, my home
to look after, friends who are worried about me.''

His mouth settled into a grim, intractable line.
''You have no choice but to wait for Captain Biggins.''

A brandied fog enveloped her brain. ''But I—''

''You are different from this afternoon when I carried you in from the beach.'' His expression softened.

She was not too drunk to notice his change of subject.

''When you ordered me locked in my room?'' She
smiled to lessen the mockery of her words. He'd be
more inclined to help if she didn't antagonize him.

When he returned her smile, a strange fluttering
developed beneath her ribs, and she swallowed a generous swig of brandy to hide her confusion.

''So I did. It appears Mrs. Givens ignored my instructions.'' Her host looked at his glass as if surprised to find it empty, then gazed at her again, tenderness gleaming in his amber eyes. ''You were so
weak and battered, we feared you might not survive.
You have a resilient spirit.''

His wide mouth curved upward in another smile,
and warmth radiated from her forehead to her bare
toes.

Cameron took her empty glass, refilled it, and
handed it back. Her fingers brushed his when she took
the glass, and his skin tingled with warmth where she

touched him. He had reacted that way toward Clarissa at first, and disaster had followed. If he learned more about this Celia, he might find her less enchanting. "Was there anyone else with you when the storm destroyed your ship?"

She shook her head. "I usually sail alone. That's when I do most of my thinking."

He felt himself drowning in the whirlpools of blue that stared up at him, while she traced the rim of her snifter with a slender index finger tipped with a pale pink nail.

"And what do you think about?" he asked.

A rosy blush suffused her skin above the lace-trimmed collar of her gown, and a delicate blue vein pulsed at her throat. "Problem-solving, mostly."

Like a sneak attack, a desire to protect her from all dilemmas surged through him. "What kind of problems?"

She lifted her chin and narrowed her eyes in a determined squint. "Nothing that can't be solved by returning home immediately."

An illogical stab of jealousy pierced him. "Is there someone waiting for you?"

Her blush deepened. "My parents are dead, and I have no other family."

"No one who misses you?"

Celia bit back her reply. Would she endanger herself by admitting no one would miss her if she didn't return immediately? Her friends would think she was hiding out, ashamed to show her face until the scandal of running away from her wedding had died down.

At first, her clients would believe she was on her honeymoon, as scheduled.

"There are those who'll search for me if I don't return home soon," she lied.

"Where do you live?" Cameron's golden gaze seemed to penetrate her deception.

She hesitated, but could think of no reason why her residence should be a secret. "Clearwater Beach."

"Clearwater Beach?"

"It's in the center of the state on the Gulf Coast."

His eyebrows arched in surprise. "You're a long way from home."

"Judging from your accent, so are you."

His eyes glittered with irony. Or was it madness? He was like no one she had ever met.

Marooned with a madman jumped unbidden into her mind.

It sounded like the title of a B-horror flick. She giggled as hysteria closed in. To calm herself, she chugged the remaining brandy in her glass.

He must have seen her distress, because he set down his glass. "You must be exhausted. You should be in bed."

That statement seemed reasonable enough. Except for his refusal to take her to the mainland, he didn't *act* crazy. If she hadn't drunk so much brandy, she could think straight. God, what was happening to her? And why hadn't she kept a clear head to deal with it?

Before she could protest, Cameron swept her off the sofa and into his arms. The hard warmth of his body pressed through the thin fabric of her gown, and involuntarily her arms reached up to twine around his neck.

Who was crazy now?

Her dizziness returned, probably a combination of the knock on her head with too much brandy. She didn't resist when he tucked her head into the hollow of his throat where his pulse pounded and carried her into the hallway and up the stairs.

Brandy coursed like fire through her veins. In a state close to dreaming, nearer to drunkenness, she nestled deeper into Cameron's embrace. Before she drifted into unconsciousness, a scene from *Gone with the Wind* flashed through her mind of Rhett carrying Scarlett up a wide stairway.

Home, she reminded herself, *she had to get home.*

"I'll worry about that tomorrow." Her voice slurred, and the last thing she remembered was giggling at her own cleverness.

As he carried her up the stairs, Cameron sensed her breath against his throat and the softness of her body in his arms. She smelled of Mrs. Givens's frangipani soap and sunshine and an intoxicating fragrance uniquely her own. He brushed his face against her hair, clasping her to him with one arm and opening her door with the other.

Before placing her on the bed, he folded the coverlet at the foot, reluctant to draw it over her and hide the sight before him. He knelt beside the bed, drank in the details of her unconscious figure, and resisted the urge to trace a finger over her high cheekbone, down the slender column of her throat, and across her delicate shoulder.

She would stay until the supply boat arrived. Even if friends or family came searching for her, they'd not find her among the Ten Thousand Islands of Florida's southeast coast. He'd barely found the place himself the first time, even with detailed maps and the competent guidance of Captain Biggins.

Twelve weeks would give him time to convince her to keep his secrets. And for him to learn if he could trust her.

She moaned slightly in her sleep, and he drew back, fearful of waking her.

When he gazed at her again, her image wavered before him, the flawless contours of her face dissolved into Clarissa's features, and blood ran in rivers across the bed.

He buried his face in his hands, forcing the waking nightmare away, and when he looked once more, she slept peacefully, whole and unharmed. He drew the covers over her, then straightened and left.

In his own room, the imagined sound of her breathing tortured him as he paced like a caged animal. The horns of a cruel dilemma impaled him. He could not take her off the island and risk discovery, yet for her own sake, he dared not let her stay.

Dawn light illuminated the veranda outside his door before he closed his eyes to sleep.

WHEN CELIA AWOKE, sunlight streamed through the French doors of the upstairs bedroom. The pain in her head had receded to a dull ache, throbbing both from her injury and her host's generosity with his brandy. Her encounter with Cameron Alexander the night before seemed like a dream. She'd been sound asleep when he tucked her into bed, so she remembered nothing after he'd carried her up the stairs.

The problem of getting off the island still faced her.

Using the basin and pitcher of water on the dresser, she washed her face, then inspected the garments Mrs. Givens must have left for her. The clothes were not only too big, which she expected, considering the plumpness of their owner, but lacked any sense of style. In addition to the skirt and blouse, she found a shapeless chemise, a slip and a pair of ruffled drawers.

She shrugged off the nightgown, stepped into the strange panties and pulled the drawstring on the voluminous drawers taut, noting the tiny, even handstitching. Mrs. Givens apparently made all her clothes since Cameron Alexander probably wouldn't let his housekeeper leave the island to shop. How did one order underwear from a charter boat captain?

Celia shook her head at her dilemma. The sooner she returned to the mainland, the sooner she could end this crazy nightmare.

She rejected the too large chemise and heavy slip—the Florida climate was too hot for either—and slipped on the gathered skirt, which hung just above her ankles. She pulled on the blouse, roomy enough for two, tied the shirttail into a knot at her waist, and rolled the long sleeves above her elbows.

After plaiting her hair into a loose French braid, she hurried down to the kitchen, determined to find Cameron and force or cajole him—whichever it took—to take her to Key West.

Chapter Two

The house looked bigger in the morning light. Double
doors at each end of the hallways and in every room
opened to the cooling winds, and the broad, encircling
roof of the veranda shaded every window. From the
dogtrot, Celia noted the house was built on stilts to
allow breezes and high water to circulate beneath, just
like many of the homes on her own Clearwater Beach.

When she entered the kitchen, Mrs. Givens looked
up from her baking. The housekeeper's mouth
dropped as her gaze traveled upward from Celia's
bare feet and ankles, exposed by the skirt, to the strip
of midriff where she'd tied the blouse above her
waistline, to her cleavage where she'd folded back the
high-necked blouse for coolness.

The older woman's cheeks glowed pink, probably
from the heat of the open hearth, and her tongue
tripped on her words. "Very pretty you are, m'dear,
and looking less like flotsam every day."

"Thanks for lending me these clothes."

"Well, now, you couldn't have worn that wedding

gown, even if it was still in one piece, could you? Not in this heat.''

Curiosity glimmered in the older woman's eyes, but Celia wasn't ready to discuss her hasty flight from the church. Mrs. Seffner's visit and her accusations against Darren seemed like a distant nightmare, one Celia wished she could forget. She wondered how Darren had taken being jilted at the altar. Had he slunk away in disgrace? Expressed concern and organized a search? Or, if he was really the murderer Mrs. Seffner believed him to be, would he attempt to track Celia down for vengeance? The possibility made her shiver in the warm air.

"Sit yourself down," Mrs. Givens said. "Your breakfast is ready."

Celia settled at one end of a large wooden table whose battered, well-scrubbed surface smelled of lemons. Mrs. Givens poured steaming coffee from an enamel pot, filled Celia's plate with scrambled eggs, grits and sliced mangoes, and moved a basket of hot rolls and a pot of honey within her reach.

Celia discovered her appetite had returned. Besides, she'd need her strength to find a way off the island. While she ate, she gazed through the open doorway of the kitchen. The island apparently was a narrow key with the Gulf of Mexico beyond the dunes to the west, and to the south and east, a bay, dotted with islands, stretched off toward the dark green mass of the mainland.

The house would have only a tenuous anchorage on the slender strip of land during a violent storm like the one that had wrecked the Morgan. Her hands trembled at the memory, and a suffocating sense of panic squeezed the air from her throat. She gulped coffee, and the scalding liquid doused the terrifying recollections of the storm and eased her breathing.

"What's this island called?" she asked, anxious to push her memories of the storm aside.

"It isn't named on any map, but Mr. Alexander calls it Solitaire."

Celia shuddered. The name evoked haunting images of a place withdrawn from society, forgotten by the world, almost as if suspended in time, like a place of legend. Its disquieting stillness made the name an apt one.

"I'd hoped after six years of Solitaire, he'd be ready to return to England." Sadness clouded Mrs. Givens's green eyes as she added eggs and butter to a bowl and began mixing with a wooden spoon. "But the longer he's here, the more determined he is to stay. I'm afraid his exile might last forever."

Celia pictured the golden stranger with the classically handsome face and a body like a Greek god. Who was this Cameron Alexander? She needed to know more about him if she was to persuade him to help end her own exile.

"What did he do in England?"

Mrs. Givens's head snapped up, and her green eyes narrowed. "Do? What do you mean?"

"What kind of work did he do?" Whatever it was, Celia mused, he must have been successful to have purchased his own island worth millions in the Florida real estate market.

Mrs. Givens laughed with a nervous twittering sound. "He was a gentleman landowner with farms, mines and such."

His work didn't sound ominous enough to make him run away to a deserted island. Maybe the illness Mrs. Givens had mentioned had caused his early retirement. "Why did he leave all that behind?"

The housekeeper ceased her stirring and set the mixing bowl down with a heavy thud. Pain contorted her face. "I am never to speak a word about that. And you mustn't ask. Mr. Alexander has sworn me not to speak of it."

"You hinted yesterday that he's ill." The night before Cameron had appeared strong and healthy, suffering only from the effects of too much brandy and his peculiar insistence that she remain on the island.

"Aye, so I did. Suffice it to say his illness is one of the heart, and let it go at that. I've said too much already."

An illness of the heart? Of the head, more likely, if he believed he could hold her hostage for three months. Celia gauged the set of the housekeeper's mouth and decided further questions would be futile.

An illness of the heart. Had an ill-fated love affair broken his grasp on reality? It must have been a grand passion to keep him on his island called Solitaire, isolated from the world and its conveniences and pleasures.

She finished her breakfast and left Mrs. Givens to

her baking. She would find Cameron Alexander and demand he take her to the mainland, even if she had to bribe him with more money than she could afford.

She stepped off the veranda and headed toward the beach. Cabbage palms provided the house's only shade, and the tropical sun beat mercilessly on the tin roof. In the dazzling white heat of late morning, not even a condensation trail from a Miami-bound jet marred the perfection of the bright sky. The name *Solitaire* fit the isolated place.

As she walked north, she discovered a huge pile of driftwood, palm fronds and flotsam someone had cleared from the beach and stacked to be burned. She recalled seeing a box of matches on a kitchen shelf. If Cameron refused to take her to Key West, she'd watch for a passing boat and light a bonfire to signal it. Pleasure boats and fishing crafts filled the Florida waters. Surely one of them would respond to the blaze and pluck her off the island.

A hand touched her shoulder, and she jumped. She'd heard no one approach, but the dark figure of Noah stood beside her, outlined by the sun.

"Howdy, miss. I saw you standing all by yourself. This place seems powerful lonesome when you first come here. I remember."

For a moment she could see her own unhappiness reflected in the man's soft brown eyes.

"Thought you might like somebody to talk to, and I'd be mighty proud to show you my garden."

"You're right. I *was* feeling lonesome."

Glad for his company, she walked down the beach

beside him. When they reached the path leading back to the house, Cameron was nowhere in sight, but Mrs. Givens was hanging linens out to dry on a line stretched between two palms behind the kitchen.

Abruptly the house appeared to waver and fade, blending into the surrounding foliage until it seemed to disappear. Celia blinked in disbelief, then squeezed her eyes shut and shook her head to dispel what must have been another touch of vertigo. When she looked again, the house stood solidly before her, its cypress clapboards bleached the pale gray of driftwood by the sun. Lush vines of magenta bougainvillea twined around its stilts and along the balustrades, softening its strong lines. It seemed such a natural part of the island, the illusion that it had disappeared must have been a trick of sunlight and heat, like a mirage in the desert.

Cameron Alexander had chosen his exile well. From a distant boat, the house would be indistinguishable among the lush vegetation of the key.

She followed Noah around the house to the island's eastern side, where he pointed with pride to his garden, heavy with vegetables, pineapples and papayas. Orange trees with dark, shining leaves and golden globes of fruit and mango and avocado trees formed a wind break along the garden's northern border. On the south side, a small outbuilding provided shelter for a cow and nesting hens.

A sea breeze rustled the palms, gulls cried overhead, and bay water lapped against a labyrinth of mangrove roots that ringed the eastern shore. Under other circumstances, Solitaire could be paradise.

"Noah, would you take me to Key West? It can't be that long a trip, and I'd pay you well for your trouble."

Fear gleamed in the man's eyes. "Not me. I don't dare go near the place."

"Why?"

"I just can't, that's all."

He avoided looking her in the eye, and she realized, like Cameron, Noah had secrets of his own. He was a huge, powerful man. She wouldn't risk angering him by asking personal questions. "I must return to my business as soon as possible. Do you think I can talk Mr. Alexander into taking me?"

Noah shook his head. "Uh-uh. Won't nothing make Mr. Alex go where they's people."

Frustration engulfed her. Her shop stood closed and empty on a street thronged with tourists, but no one would miss her. Her customers would think she was on her honeymoon. With her parents dead, she had no other close relatives, no one to alert the Coast Guard to search for her when she didn't return home. Tracey knew Celia had often taken the sailboat out for days at a time. Her friend wouldn't be worried yet, especially since she knew Celia would be embarrassed about skipping out on her own wedding. Tracey would probably guess she was lying low until the brouhaha blew over.

"Won't do much good," Noah said, "but you can try asking Mr. Alex."

"But I can't find him! Where can he hide on an island?"

Noah pointed to a break in the mangroves where a dock stretched out into the bay. Beyond it, a white sail flashed on the water as a boat tacked toward the island. Celia squared her shoulders and headed toward the dock for a showdown with her mysterious host.

CAMERON TURNED HIS sailboat north toward the island, where his thoughts had been drawn all morning, no matter how hard he had tried to escape them. Always before, his excursions among the hundreds of small islands helped scour away the painful memories of his past, renewing his spirit and his strength. But everything had changed with the storm that brought Celia Stevens to his beach. What little peace he had wrested from his exile seemed lost to him forever.

She haunted him everywhere he looked. The gulf waters sparkled and shone like her eyes. Her melodic voice murmured in the breeze. The swaying of tall palms mimicked her movements, and the sea oats fringing the dunes glistened as bright as her hair. His conversation with her had been brief, but long enough to recognize the intelligence behind her beautiful face. Damn her! The woman had no obvious faults, gave him no ammunition to resist her.

And resist he must—for twelve long weeks until Captain Biggins and the supply boat arrived to take her away. And then only after he'd sworn her to secrecy about his whereabouts, not only for his own safety but for hers.

He toyed briefly with the idea of sending Noah to take her to Key West, but he could not place the man who had served him so faithfully in such peril. If Noah was arrested, his spirit would wither and die. God knew, Cameron would take her there himself, if he dared, but the risk of discovery was too great.

And what about the risk to her?

He grappled with his conscience as he adjusted the lines of the sail. Celia Stevens was much safer on the island with Mrs. Givens and Noah to protect her than alone on the open sea with him.

And how would he survive twelve weeks with her reminding him of all he had lost? He steered the boat onto the nearest sandbar, dropped anchor and dove overboard fully clothed in a futile attempt to drown the anguish that consumed him.

CELIA WALKED DOWN THE sandy path toward the dock. With his strange reclusiveness, Cameron might turn and sail away again if he saw her, so she stepped off the path and into the covering shade of the mangroves to await his arrival.

The sloop, its white sail shimmering in the sun like the wing of a giant gull, glided across the smooth green waters of the bay. The boat tacked, and the sail shifted to its port side, exposing Cameron at the tiller. With his bare feet propped against one side of the boat, his hair blowing in the wind, and the look of pleasure illuminating the handsome planes of his face, thrown back to catch the full blast of the blazing sun, he erased the image of an unhappy recluse with an unsound mind that she'd carried with her all morning.

The ripple of muscles beneath his tanned skin, revealed by his shirt flapping open in the breeze and slacks rolled to his knees, projected a vibrancy and power that made him seem one with the elements of wind and water surrounding him. Her confidence ebbed when she considered coercing the dynamic being before her into doing anything he didn't want to do.

As the boat neared the dock, Cameron lowered the sail, and the craft slid silently toward the shore. He tossed a line around a piling with the easy grace of long experience, pulled the boat alongside the dock, and levered himself on strong arms with corded muscles up onto the pier, where he tied the boat fast.

She stepped out of the mangroves and onto the dock behind him. He straightened from tying up the lines, and, at over six feet tall, would tower above her. His height made him appear even more threatening, but she gathered her courage and called to him. ''Mr. Alexander, I need to talk with you.''

He turned at her call, and his voice rolled like thunder up the pier. ''You should know better than to sneak up on a man like that.''

Undaunted, she stepped forward. The hot, weathered wood seared her bare feet. If he thought he could bully her, he was in for a surprise. She straightened her shoulders, thrust her chin high, and walked toward the giant who stood glaring at her with topaz eyes.

''I instructed Mrs. Givens to tell you that I wanted

to be left alone." The bitterness in his voice lashed out at her, and she hesitated.

Where was the gentle man who had carried her to her bed the night before? Was this alter personality a sign of his mental instability?

She came within a few feet of him, close enough to read his expression and block his exit from the dock, but not so close she had to crane her neck to look up at him. To crack the barrier his anger erected, she smiled her sweetest smile, but his stony grimace didn't waver.

She changed tactics and attempted to appear businesslike. "Mrs. Givens told me you want to be left alone. That's what I want to talk to you about."

His expression didn't change, nor did he speak. He stood like a colossus with his bare feet planted squarely upon the pier and his balled fists upon his hips while the sun beat down on him.

A trickle of perspiration slid between her breasts. She wouldn't allow him to intimidate her. She had too much at stake. "I must return home immediately, and I'd be very grateful if you'd take me as far as Key West in your boat."

"No." He didn't bellow this time, but spoke in a soft, low voice. His cool, intractable tone disturbed her more than his yelling had.

"Why not? It's a reasonable request." She hoped her voice didn't reveal the trembling she felt inside.

His hard frown turned to an icy look. "I'm sorry, but I owe you no explanation. I said *no,* and *no* is what I mean."

He took a step toward her, but she held her ground. "If you really want to be left alone, you'd jump at the chance to be rid of me as soon as possible."

She waited, but received no response. His strange, golden eyes weren't focused on her face but at the thin fabric of her blouse, pulled taut over her bare breasts. His strange expression drew a blush to her face and sent a tremor through her stomach. His face flushed beneath his tan, and he jerked his gaze to a point past her shoulder.

She trembled at his reaction. Cameron might be crazy, but he was a man, after all, one who hadn't seen a woman other than Mrs. Givens in years. All the more reason to leave his island as quickly as possible.

"While I appreciate your hospitality," she said, striving to maintain her reasonable tone, "I don't want to intrude on it for twelve weeks. A quick trip to Key West would solve both our problems."

"Miss Stevens." His soft, controlled voice projected menace and power. "I will say this only once more, so be convinced that I mean it. I will *not* take you to Key West."

She dreaded staying on the island more than she feared his anger. "Then tell Noah to take me."

"You can travel there on the supply boat in twelve weeks."

"As I said, I can't wait—"

"I'm sorry, but you have no choice." His face assumed the intractable expression she recognized from the previous night.

Her temper snapped out of control. "You are the most arrogant, pigheaded, selfish—"

"Selfish?" His coolness irritated her. "I'm offering to house, clothe and feed you for several months. I call that hospitality, not selfishness."

"Call it what you like, but you're not doing me any favors." Tears of anger welled in her eyes, and she dashed them away with the back of her hand, furious she'd allowed him to witness her distress, and even more furious when it failed to move him.

His expression remained unchanged. "That's all I have to say. Now stand aside and let me pass."

When she stepped quickly from his path, a splinter from the rough wood of the pier drove deep into the instep of her right foot. "Ow!"

Her yell reverberated across the water, frightening an anhinga from his mangrove perch. When she lifted her foot and extracted the offending sliver, the movement overbalanced her, and she tumbled backward into the bay and plunged underwater. Panic surged within her, fueled by memories of her shipwreck that she longed to forget, but her terror was short-lived. Her feet struck bottom, and she gained a footing in the chest-high water. Muck squished between her toes as she coughed, sputtered, and pushed her streaming hair back from her face.

Cameron peered over the dockside with a fleeting expression that might have been a smile. He reached out his hands to her, and she grabbed them. Knotting the powerful muscles of his arms, he lifted her easily out of the water onto the pier. The soles of her feet were slippery with muck, and she slid against him. His arms closed around her like a vice, driving the breath from her lungs.

A shock like an electric current raced the length of her body where she molded against him, and when she tried to pull away, his embrace tightened. She pressed her hands against the broad expanse of his bare chest and pushed. The heated look in his eyes disoriented her.

What was wrong with her? Just because he had given her the shirt off his back, just because he'd rescued her with such gentleness didn't give her a reason to respond to him—especially when he refused to take her home.

She shook her head to dispel the giddiness, spraying droplets like a wet dog. When Cameron released her, water dripped from her clothing and pooled around her on the dock.

Like a man enchanted, he stared, as if looking at her was somehow painful. For a moment, time stopped as she faced him on the dock, drinking in the sight of him while his gaze swept over her. Then he turned and marched off the pier, abruptly breaking the spell.

A moment later, a door slammed and her host disappeared into the house. Now more than ever she wanted to flee Solitaire, before he—or her response to him—drew her into a situation she couldn't control.

THAT NIGHT, CLAD ONCE again in one of Mrs. Givens's voluminous nightgowns, Celia leaned against the veranda railing outside her room, watching the rain move in torrents across the dark beach. Mrs. Givens had taken away her drenched clothes to wash the bay water from them, but they wouldn't dry soon in this rain. Thunderclouds obscured the waning moon, and water beat upon the tin roof above her, drowning out the rumble of the surf.

A blinding bolt of lightning split the sky, striking so close to the house that flash and thunder occurred simultaneously. She jumped back from the railing, throwing her arms over her face in a useless gesture of protection. With the boom reverberating in her ears, her throat tightened and her heart pounded. The storm that had demolished her boat flashed back at her. Images of murky water and towering waves crowded against her consciousness, and her breath came in tortured, painful gasps.

Post-traumatic stress syndrome.

That had to be it. Every time the thunder boomed, she relived the horror of her boat breaking up beneath her and the whirlpool pulling her under. She'd encountered storms before, had even capsized in them, but nothing had ever approached the pulsing terror that had grabbed her from the deck and dragged her down into the gray-green depths, charged with the lightning that had crackled all around her.

She closed her eyes, pushed the memories away, and grasped the balustrade so tightly her nails dug crescents into the wood. Thunder crashed again, and the house shuddered from the force of its concussion.

To ward off the panic attack that threatened to engulf her, she imagined herself in Sand Castles, her bookstore with its wide, sunny windows overlooking the traffic-thronged street and flooding the broad aisles with light. She could almost smell the inky tang of new books, the fragrance of freshly brewed tea, and the spicy, chocolate aroma rising from the basket of homemade cookies she kept beside the teapot for her customers. The soft murmur of customers' voices, the rustle of turning pages, the clunk of books returned to the shelves, and the click of keys on the cash register echoed in her memory.

The familiar images calmed her. Slowly her breathing eased, and the rhythm of her heart steadied. The panic had gone, but at her own beckoning, she'd called up a homesickness as sharp as an injury.

Gradually the force of the storm passed over the island and out to sea, leaving a silence broken only by the irregular beat of water, dripping like tears from the eaves onto the papery surface of palm fronds. The air, cooled and washed by the rain, caught the folds of her gown, puffing it out like a spinnaker.

She peered down the beach where rain obscured the piles of debris. Even if a boat were to pass the island, the driftwood and palm branches would be too wet tonight to burn as signal beacons. She'd hidden beneath her mattress the matches she'd taken from the kitchen when Mrs. Givens's back was turned. The debris would eventually dry, and she'd have her chance.

She tensed at the sound of movements in the room next to hers. A pool of light spread across the ve-

randa, and the French doors of the room next to hers
swung open. For a moment, she feared Cameron himself would step onto the porch beside her.

Then his shadow fell across the veranda floor as he
removed his clothes. The lamplight projected an un-
distorted image of his powerful shoulders, narrow
waist and lean hips upon the weathered boards, faith-
ful even to the bulges of his muscled torso when he
removed his shirt. The shadow bent to blow out the
lamp, and bedsprings creaked as he climbed into bed.
Her pulse quickened at the intimacy of the sound.

She shivered when the rain-laden breeze struck her.
Had the cool air or the memory of his body against
hers caused the tremor? She hadn't reacted that way
to Darren, who had professed to love her. Why did
her rebellious body respond only to a man whose
mind was surely disturbed?

At her first chance, she'd light her signal fire, and
if that didn't bring help, she'd steal the sloop and sail
to Key West by herself. One thing was certain. She
couldn't remain much longer on this small island with
Cameron Alexander, or she might succumb to the
growing excitement that quivered in the depths of her
whenever she thought of him—a peril worse than
shipwreck.

She pulled the rocking chair from her room onto
the veranda and, hugging her knees to her chest, she
rocked herself to sleep.

DAYLIGHT WAS GATHERING, and the rising sun tinged
the gulf's soft swells an iridescent pink and gold, like

the inside of a conch shell she'd found on the beach the day before. Seabirds searched for their breakfast, and their shrill cries and the gentle beat of their wings filled the cool morning air.

She stood and stretched, easing muscles cramped from a night spent curled in the rocker in the open air. The doors to Cameron's room remained open, but no sound came from inside. As she turned toward her own room, a flash of movement on the beach drew her attention.

Bathed in the delicate glow of the sun's first rays, Cameron, his muscles etched like Italian marble against the blue of the morning sky, strode naked across the beach toward the breakers. He moved with grace and power, and once he reached the combers crashing onto the shore, dived like a gilded arrow into the waves, slicing through them with powerful strokes of his well-muscled arms. His tawny hair fanned around him like seaweed as he swam toward the distant horizon.

Fascinated by the work of art in the flesh before her, she stood awestruck, hypnotized, watching him cut his way through the water, farther and farther from shore.

A glimpse of white on the horizon beyond him caught her eye. Moving slowly northward, so far away it looked like a child's toy, sailed a cruise ship.

Rescuers!

She didn't understand her strong reactions to her mysterious host and felt the need to get away from him as strongly as she wanted to go home.

She darted back into her room and rummaged under the mattress for the stolen matches. With the precious sticks clutched in her fist, she dashed headlong down the stairs, through the wide front doors, and out toward the beach.

She raced between the dunes and headed north along the shoreline. She had to ignite the signal fire before the ship passed from view, but deep sand sucked at her feet, slowing her progress.

When she reached the stack of debris, she cast about for a hard surface on which to strike a match. Shaking with excitement until she could barely grasp the matchstick, she grabbed a large shell with a corrugated surface and dragged the match across it.

Nothing happened.

In a panic, she drew the match again and again across the shell's rough surface, but it didn't flare.

Dear God, make it burn, so I can go home.

She threw the match down in disgust and tried another. The second flared instantly, and she touched it to the dried palm fronds stacked with the flotsam and jetsam. Still slightly damp from the earlier rain, they smoldered slowly, producing little heat or smoke. She pulled one of the fronds from the pile and fanned, coaxing the smoldering leaves into flames.

With an explosive burst, the dry palm branches on the bottom of the pile caught fire, and flames licked along the driftwood and other debris. She peered toward the horizon, tracking the cruise liner, and fanned harder, encouraging the flames to burn brighter.

Out of nowhere, strong hands tugged her aside. She

stumbled and fell to her knees on the beach. Sand flew like dust devils, obscuring her view.

She scrambled to her feet and wiped sand from her eyes. Cameron, barefoot and clad only in jeans unbuttoned at the waist, stood where she had been, using a board as a shovel to douse the last embers of the fire with sand.

"No!" The word tore from her throat, and she grabbed his arm. "Let it burn. That boat *must* see it."

He pushed her aside once again and continued heaping sand on the debris.

She thrust herself between him and the fire, trying to block the sand from her precious flames. "You have no right to stop me!"

"Stay out of the way!"

She ignored his warning and dug at the sand he had heaped upon the debris, but her efforts were useless against the power of the man. For every handful of sand she uncovered, he shoveled piles more onto the fire and her as well.

When he'd smothered every spark, he dropped the board and dusted his hands. Water glistened in his tawny hair, and anger gleamed in his eyes.

When he turned to her, he did not meet her gaze, but cast his glance at a point behind her. "You must impress this fact into that very pretty head of yours, Miss Stevens. You will leave this island when I say, and not before."

He snatched the remaining matches from her clenched fist. She grabbed instinctively to retrieve them, but his dark expression stopped her. He turned and tramped back toward the house, leaving her shivering with disappointment and the first rumblings of fear as she stood on the beach with her nightgown billowing in the wind.

She was no longer a guest on Solitaire, but a prisoner.

Chapter Three

Celia stood like a sentinel, staring toward the northwest until the last sight of the cruise liner disappeared over the horizon. Her hope vanished with it, and she headed back toward the house. Deep sand pulled at her feet, as if the earth itself tried to chain her to the island.

When she reached the path through the dunes, she met Noah loping toward the shore with a shovel across his shoulder.

"Morning, miss." He smiled, but his deep, dark eyes held their usual sadness, and she wondered if he was as much a prisoner in this place as she was.

"You're out early," she said. "Digging for coquina?"

"No, ma'am, though some good coquina stew would taste mighty fine. Mr. Alex wants me to bury that pile of trash on the north beach. Don't want it calling attention to the place, he says."

"Right." Her smile froze as Noah passed her on the path.

When she reached the house, Cameron lounged on

his elbows on the wide stairs that led to the veranda. He had pulled on a shirt, but his chest and feet remained bare, and his hair had begun to dry into a wild, disarrayed mass. On another man, the effect would have been scruffiness. On Cameron, Celia thought with a sigh, his disheveled appearance made him all the more attractive, like a sexy male model in a Calvin Klein ad.

He sprang to his feet at her approach, but she'd had her fill of rudeness for one morning. She attempted to climb the stairs past him.

"Miss Stevens, please." The desperation in his eyes stopped her.

"What is it now? Want to search me for more matches?" Ignoring how attractive he looked, she centered all her fury and frustration in her voice.

Standing above him on the steps with her eyes level with his, she could read the silent appeal in them, as well as the pleading gesture of his hands spread wide.

"Forgive me, please. I meant you no harm, but I had to extinguish the fire as quickly as possible."

Her anger dissolved into smothering depression, and her voice lost its snap and turned thick and heavy. "What harm would it have done for that ship to see the flames and come take me away from here?"

She sank onto the stairs with her elbows on her knees and her chin tucked in her hands. The dragging weight of her body mirrored the heaviness of her spirit. She dredged up the energy to speak again. "I have a home, friends, a business I want to return to."

She had made the plea so many times, it sounded

like a litany. She tried to will her tears away, but they slid down her cheeks, and she tasted their saltiness.

Cameron settled onto the step beside her, placed his arm around her shoulders, and drew her toward him. The gentle man beside her had no correlation to the angry being who had pushed her away from the fire only moments before. Was the illness Mrs. Givens had referred to a split personality?

"Please don't cry." His voice caressed her with its warmth.

"I'm not crying." She swiped her tears with the back of her hand and pulled away from him.

"Tell me," he said, "are you anxious to return because of the man you were to marry?"

His question stunned her. The last person she wanted to see was Darren Walker, but if Cameron could keep his secrets, so could she. "I don't know what you're talking about."

An engaging smile tugged at the corners of his mouth. "My situation here is strange, I admit. However, no stranger than yours. How many women go sailing alone dressed in a wedding gown?"

Embarrassed, she gazed silently past him toward the gulf.

"Did you sail before or after the wedding?"

"Why should you care?" she asked hotly.

He shrugged with infuriating nonchalance.

"If I answer," she said, "will you let me leave?"

His smile vanished. "You may leave when Captain Biggins comes to take you home."

"But Captain Biggins won't be here for weeks!

And why is it okay for *him* to take me off the island, but no one else? What are you trying to hide?''

Cameron stared at her as if he hadn't heard. He spoke in a strangely detached voice, as if talking to himself. ''Your eyes are the color of the gulf on a sunny day, and when you're angry, they flash like sunlight on the water.''

Her anger turned to alarm. The man *was* crazy. ''You're avoiding my question. Why is it that Biggins—''

''You asked what I'm trying to hide. The answer is obvious.''

''Not to me—''

''I am hiding myself.''

''Why?''

His face shifted into hard lines. ''That's none of your affair. More to the point, I've spent years guarding the location of my hideaway. Biggins is the only person on earth who knows where I am.''

''You must trust him a great deal.''

''As long as he keeps my secret, Biggins is a very wealthy man. If he divulges my presence here, his money stops. It is as simple as that.''

She started to ask again why he was hiding but bit back the words. Knowing too much might be dangerous. He'd just indirectly informed her that when she left Solitaire, the number of people who knew his whereabouts would double. *If* he allowed her to leave. Her doubts on that score were multiplying by the minute.

She had no intention of waiting for Captain Biggins. She had promised earlier she would reach the mainland if she had to swim, and she meant it. She refused to spend another night on Solitaire.

Everything about her mysterious host was odd, and at the same time, somehow compelling, drawing her to him. She'd just escaped one disastrous relationship and didn't need—or want—another. The more distance she could place between her and Solitaire's enigmatic owner, the better off she'd be.

She jumped to her feet and started up the stairs, but Cameron grasped her hand, holding her fast. His expression softened again, and his lip curved in a rueful smile. "Don't go."

"I must dress."

"But you haven't forgiven me for treating you so roughly on the beach. I *am* sorry."

Did Cameron think he could behave like a jerk, then make everything all right by apologizing? "I'll forgive you, but only when you free me from this island prison you've built for yourself."

She wrenched her hand from his grasp, lifted her gown to her knees, raced into the house and up the stairs to her room.

Still warm from Mrs. Givens's iron, the skirt and blouse she'd worn the day before when she'd plunged into the bay lay across the bed. She considered them with a sigh. She had to get off the island, if for no other reason than to find clothes that fit and a decent pair of shoes.

"Excuse me."

She turned at Cameron's voice and saw him standing at the open door. "What do you want?"

"Noah found a backpack washed onto the beach yesterday. These were in it, and I believe they're from the wreckage of your boat. Mrs. Givens took the liberty of laundering them."

Cameron offered her the bundle in his arms. Folded neatly were the extra set of clothes she'd kept on board the boat. Denim shorts, a T-shirt, bra and panties, and a pair of sneakers.

She took the clothes from him. "Thank you."

"If there's anything else you need, we'll do our best to provide it for you."

"What is this, a four-star prison?" She couldn't keep the sarcasm from her voice.

His expression hardened, and he turned and left. She was instantly sorry she had insulted him when he was only trying to be kind. However, she couldn't allow herself to be taken in by his seductive charm. Whatever else the attractive Cameron Alexander was, he was also her jailer.

She washed the sand from her body and dressed in the skirt and blouse. She brushed the grit from her hair, smoothing her tangled curls, and stepped out onto the veranda as she braided her hair.

Down the beach, Noah scooped great shovels of sand onto a mound beside the gaping hole in which he stood, looking like a gravedigger as he bent to his task.

The sight sobered her and strengthened her resolve to leave that day. She began to form her plan.

WHEN CELIA ENTERED THE kitchen for breakfast, Mrs. Givens was examining a length of leaf-green fabric.

"We must make you some clothes, m'dear. Can't have you wearing my castoffs forever."

"Forever?" Celia stopped pouring coffee and looked at the woman.

"It's just a figure of speech," the housekeeper replied a bit too quickly, "although I suppose at your young age several weeks seem like a lifetime."

Her explanation sounded sensible enough, but Celia couldn't shake her uneasy feeling about the island and its inhabitants. For all their protestations of wanting to be left alone, their concerted refusal to let her leave frightened her.

More resolved to escape than ever, she finished filling her cup and helped herself to a generous serving of thick oatmeal and toast. She'd need nourishment to carry out her plan.

"Mrs. Givens, would you have time to pack me a lunch? I think I'll wander the beach and collect shells today." She spooned marmalade onto the toast, trying to act unruffled while her heart pounded at her lies.

"Happy to, m'dear. Captain Biggins brought a nice salted ham on his last visit, and I have some biscuits I made for Mr. Alexander's breakfast."

"Could you put a bottle of water in with that, and some tea? The heat makes me thirsty."

"Whatever you want, you just let me know. I'm happy to oblige."

Mrs. Givens beamed at her, and she wondered if

the woman's happiness came from Celia's apparent reconciliation to her fate.

"You're a sweetheart." Celia smiled at the woman, who unknowingly was preparing food for her escape.

Her smile disappeared when Cameron entered the room. He looked past her as if she wasn't there. He had combed his tousled hair, shaved the stubble from his face, and put on fresh clothes. As he stood in the doorway, dressed in fitted pants tucked into gleaming boots and a soft white shirt open at the collar, he reminded her of a cover model for the paperback historical romances she had trouble keeping in stock on her bookstore shelves. Regret that she hadn't met him under different circumstances washed through her.

"Please bring my breakfast to the study," he ordered the housekeeper, "and see that I'm not disturbed this morning. I want to bring my journals up to date."

Before Mrs. Givens could reply, he was gone. Celia took a last bite of toast, then cleared her dishes from the table.

"I'll have your basket packed in two shakes of a lamb's tail," the housekeeper promised.

Celia descended the veranda stairs from the kitchen and headed toward the outbuildings where the privy stood.

Get me out of here she prayed, *and I will never take hot running water and flushing toilets for granted ever again.*

Before entering, she carefully checked the small structure for spiders and snakes.

When she exited the outbuilding, she glanced beyond the garden. Cameron's sailboat lay tied to the pier.

So far, so good.

She returned to the kitchen, collected the basket Mrs. Givens had filled with enough food for two, and crept past the study and up the stairs to her room. There she removed Mrs. Givens's skirt and blouse, pulled on her shorts and T-shirt, and tied her sneakers. From the veranda, she could see Noah, still excavating sand on the beach.

She retrieved her basket and hurried downstairs, past the closed doors that sheltered Cameron, and out the front door.

Mrs. Givens was belting out a hymn in the kitchen as she worked. Celia darted through the garden and onto the pier. The tide was in, the boat rode high in the water, and she climbed easily on board and cast off the lines.

She shoved the sailboat away from the dock, raised the mainsail, and guided the boat north. The sails captured the wind, and the boat skimmed along the water between Solitaire and a key to the east, out of sight of the house and of Noah on the beach. When another key blocked Solitaire from view, she sailed west into the open waters of the gulf.

Both Cameron and Mrs. Givens had said Key West was the closest town, but she couldn't be certain. Without instruments or a radio, she feared that if she headed south, she'd steer too far west and end up in

Cuba or head across the gulf toward the Yucatán peninsula.

Even if Solitaire was at the southernmost tip of the state, a day's sailing north along the coast should bring her at least as far as Everglades City, where she could hire a fishing guide to return Cameron's boat, and, more important, rent a car to drive home.

She panicked for a moment when she realized she had no money or credit cards, then breathed easier as she remembered her bank had branches all over the state, and with her memorized account number, she could withdraw the funds she'd need. She threw back her head, drinking in the sunshine, salt air, and the taste of freedom. After a harrowing few days, everything was going to work out all right.

If Cameron should attempt to come after her in the skiff she had noticed along the shore, he'd probably head south, thinking she'd struck out for Key West. By the time he realized she'd traveled in the opposite direction, she'd be on Interstate 75, halfway home to Clearwater.

She continued north, maintaining a course parallel to the shoreline that marked the western edge of the Everglades, but keeping far enough out to avoid sandbars. After raising the jib, she settled back in the stern, guiding the tiller with one hand, while she raided Mrs. Givens's picnic basket with the other for a ripe, sweet mango. Running before the wind, the sloop sliced through the aquamarine waters. If the breeze held, she should reach civilization near sundown.

Her only companions were the gulls that swooped

to land on the deck, hoping for a crumb from her basket, the frigate birds circling on the air currents high above and a trio of porpoises that played in the boat's wake. The sky seemed bluer, the water clearer, and the fish and birds more bountiful than she had ever seen them. She attributed her increased awareness of the beauty of nature to her earlier brush with death and today's heady taste of freedom.

Surrounded by glorious peacefulness, she thought back to the reason she'd sailed off into the gulf a few days before. She'd needed time and space to decide what to do about Darren.

As soon as she returned home, she would contact the police and tell them of Mrs. Seffner's accusations. In the meantime, she could only pray Darren wouldn't be waiting on her doorstep, demanding an explanation.

Or, worse yet, prepared to exact revenge for his embarrassment and his loss of her inheritance. She could recall now flashes of temper that he'd managed to keep under control during their engagement. Would her run from the church have pushed him over the edge to violence?

Suddenly the joy vanished from the day. She was sailing from one problem straight into the arms of another.

Thinking of arms, she recalled Cameron Alexander and the excitement his touch had sent coursing through her when she'd stumbled against him on the dock yesterday. Darren had never affected her that way. She'd been attracted to Darren because he'd seemed safe and predictable.

Cameron Alexander was neither.

No matter. Both men would be history soon enough, with Cameron hidden away on Solitaire, and Darren, she hoped, out of her life for good. With her rotten track record with men, maybe she should become an old maid, devoting her life to her bookstore, wearing long black dresses, her hair in a bun and gold-rimmed reading glasses. She'd adopt an aloof, overweight cat to complete her image.

The wind changed, snatching the sail and threatening to capsize the boat. Maybe she should just pay attention to her sailing.

The sun dropped closer to the horizon. She had finished the food in the basket and drunk the tea and water, but she had yet to see any signs of civilization. What she did see filled her with apprehension. The sky had turned a sickly green and filled with ominous cumulus thunderheads. A storm was brewing. October was part of the peak hurricane season in Florida. Celia hadn't heard a weather forecast in days, and for all she knew, the clouds bearing down on her now could be a tropical storm.

Or a hurricane.

She cut her course closer to shore, hoping to catch a glimpse of a fishing camp where she could take shelter.

"Damn you, Cameron Alexander," she yelled into the growing wind, "if you'd taken me to Key West as I asked you, I'd be in a car on my way home now instead of stranded in a storm.''

The longer she searched for a place to ride out the storm, the greater her anger grew.

''*You* needn't have stayed in Key West,'' she shouted above the snap of the sails. ''You could've just dropped me off and gone on your way. How much trouble would that have been, you golden-eyed, muscle-bound—''

A ferocious downdraft of wind caught the sails, heeled the boat to its side, and jerked the words from her mouth as she pitched into the turbulent water.

CAMERON STRUGGLED TO concentrate on his journals. He hadn't brought them up to date since before the storm that had washed Celia Stevens onto his beach. He couldn't erase her lovely face from his mind or deny his admiration for her pluck and courage. Women he had known in London would have taken to their beds for months after experiencing what she'd been through. But she had raised her chin and stiffened her back and refused to admit defeat. Would she resign herself to circumstances before Captain Biggins arrived or continue to fight him every step of the way?

The door to his study flew open and banged against the wall. Mrs. Givens stood on the threshold as if the hounds of hell were at her heels.

''What is it?'' he said. ''Have I been discovered? Are the authorities here?''

"It's the girl." Her face glowed red above her apron, and he feared for her health.

"Sit down and catch your breath." He went to her, took her arm, and led her to the leather armchair by the window. "Now, what about the girl?"

"She's gone." Mrs. Givens gasped for air.

"Gone? Where could she go?" Had the long years of exile affected his housekeeper's mind? "It's impossible for her to leave the island."

"Indeed it is possible, sir. She stole your boat."

"What?" Anger washed over him along with the embarrassing realization that he'd underestimated Celia Stevens.

"I looked up from my baking and saw the sail moving out across the bay. I ran down to the pier, thinking I could call her back, but by the time I reached the water, she'd disappeared behind the next key." The housekeeper panted for air, fanning her heated face with her apron.

Disaster had stalked him once more, but perhaps he could yet triumph. He would need sail power to catch up with her. "Tell Noah to bring the extra canvas. I'll rig a sail for the skiff and follow her to Key West."

But Mrs. Givens didn't move. She sat, gasping for breath and shaking her head. "No, no."

"No! Do you want her to get away?" Anger and frustration erupted as he thundered at the woman.

"She's not headed for Key West. She went north."

He grinned at Celia's resourcefulness. "She hoped to throw us off her trail."

He raced to the veranda, bellowed at Noah to meet him at the shed, and sprinted across the garden to the outbuilding. Together they gathered tackle, canvas and lines and carried them to the dock to rig the skiff.

Cameron's hands shook as he worked. With her lead, he might never catch her. The coast stretched north for over a hundred miles of wilderness. He had little hope of finding her, the proverbial needle in a haystack.

But he had to try. He couldn't allow her to disclose his location. And, if anything happened to her, the blame was his. If he hadn't refused to take her to Key West, she wouldn't have taken flight.

Mrs. Givens thrust a basket of food and water into the skiff and he shoved off, steering north along the coast. When daylight faded and a storm approached, he sailed on into the gloom, hoping for a glimpse of white sail. With the thousands of keys and tiny islets along the coastline, he could pass within a hundred yards of her and miss her altogether.

And if lost among the Ten Thousand Islands, she died of exposure and dehydration, he would have yet another death on his conscience. Even his self-imposed exile could not atone for that. He sailed on into the night, trimming his sails against the gathering storm, and searching every shoreline for signs of the sailboat. Twice, unable to judge the water's depth in the darkness, he ran aground on sandbars. Twice he climbed out into the waves to push the skiff free.

Ready to admit defeat in the pitch-black gloom, he

caught sight of a huge white form, floating in the water and partially hidden by a nearby key. With a sinking heart, he recognized his sailboat.

But he saw no sign of Celia Stevens.

Chapter Four

In the pitch darkness of the storm with waves pounding his tiny craft, Cameron fought to guide the skiff around the tiny island of mangroves and closer to his sailboat awash in the breakers. He'd have missed the capsized boat altogether if it hadn't been illuminated by a brilliant flash of lightning.

Cupping his hands to his mouth, he yelled, "Miss Stevens! Are you out there?"

The howling wind snatched his words away and drowned them in booming thunder. If he was going to locate the woman, he had no choice but to wait for the storm to pass.

With a gaff hook, he grabbed a loose line from the sailboat and tied it to the skiff. Then he furled his canvas, dropped anchor and prepared to ride out the gale. His hopes for finding Celia diminished with the wind, and his conscience rebuked him for his treatment of her. He'd been selfish, just as she'd accused him. How could she know that his selfishness was the only thing that had kept him alive these past six years?

His rationalization brought him little comfort. In just a few days, he'd grown fond of the woman fate had washed onto his beach, and he couldn't bear to think that she had perished in this latest storm.

The squall died, and the torrential rain abated just before sunrise. In the pale twilight before dawn, Cameron spied a piece of canvas the wind had tossed onto the mangroves along the shore. He weighed anchor, grabbed an oar, and rowed to the tiny spit of land. After beaching the skiff, he made his way over the sand to the remnant of sail, fearful that this time Celia had drowned in the storm, and if he found her at all, it would be only to bury her.

As he neared the canvas, he noted that it had landed over a mangrove branch as if to form a tent. Then he heard the distinct swat of flesh against flesh and a muttered curse.

"Blasted mosquitoes and no-see-ums," Celia's angry voice grumbled. "You're eating me alive."

Relief and happiness flooded him at the sound. "Hello!" he called.

Silence reigned for an instant, then Celia poked her head around the side of the canvas. Welcome shone briefly in her eyes before she scowled. "It's you."

He glanced around and opened his arms in a gesture that took in their surroundings. "Under these conditions, I would think you'd be glad to see me."

She clambered from beneath the sail, dusting sand from her legs and clothes. "You're the one I'm running away from."

"If you want me to leave—"

"No!" Panic tinged her voice. "I was beginning to feel like Tom Hanks."

"The actor?"

"Cast-Away," she explained, then shook her head. "I forgot. You haven't seen a movie in the last six years."

He couldn't help grinning, not only because he was elated that she was safe and well, but also at the irony of her situation. "You don't have much luck with boats, do you?"

"I'm fine with boats. Weather's the problem." She jerked up her chin and glared at him. "Even the best of sailors is little match for the storm that just passed."

He nodded, conceding her point. "What do you intend to do now?"

She narrowed her eyes and considered him warily. "Since I've come this far, I don't suppose you'd take me the rest of the way to Everglades City?"

He shook his head. "I can't do that."

She bristled with outrage. "I won't tell anyone who you are. And I couldn't find your island again if I tried, so your hideaway is safe."

"I can't take that chance."

"You mean you *won't* take it."

They were back to the same argument, one he would not allow her to win. "Are you thirsty? Hungry?"

She flicked a delectable pink tongue across dry lips. "My supplies ran out late yesterday afternoon."

Without a word, he went to the skiff, grabbed a

water bottle, Mrs. Givens's basket and a dry blanket, then returned to Celia. He spread the blanket on the sand and motioned for her to sit.

"We might as well wait," he said.

She eyed him with suspicion. "For what?"

"The tide. When the water's deeper, I'll refloat and bail out the sailboat."

She sat crosslegged on the blanket, and he handed her the water bottle. While she drank, he spread the remaining contents of the basket on a napkin and helped himself to a ham biscuit.

"You're lucky, you know," he said between bites.

"Ha!" She looked at him as if he'd lost his mind. "Held captive in the wilderness. Some luck."

"I could have missed you in the storm. How long would you have lasted out here with no water, no food and no real shelter?"

Instead of answering, she picked up a biscuit and bit into it angrily.

"Think of it this way," he said, "in three months, you'll be on your way home."

She cut her eyes toward him with an I-don't-believe-a-word-of-it look, then returned her attention to her biscuit.

After eating, he lay back on his elbows. Celia still showed no inclination to talk to him, but in spite of her chilly silence, Cameron felt the most relaxed and satisfied he'd been since before his arrival on Solitaire. He attributed his good feelings to the beautiful woman at his side. She had made his life *interesting* for the first time in years.

With a full stomach and his worries about Celia over, he was tempted to drift off to sleep, until an image of Celia commandeering his skiff and sailing away again brought him fully alert. With a sigh, he noted the incoming tide. After removing his boots and rolling up his pants legs, he waded into the surf toward the capsized boat.

CELIA REMAINED ON THE blanket, watching Cameron struggle to right and bail out the boat. She could have helped him, but she was too blasted mad. Other feelings warred within her—frustration at her aborted escape and relief that she'd been rescued.

Cameron, on the other hand, appeared to suffer no emotional pangs of any kind. He was whistling cheerfully, even while tussling with wet sails. Bad enough that he looked so damned happy. Why did he have to look so irresistibly appealing as well? With his shirt stripped off, sunlight glistened off the gleaming muscles of his chest and back. Reluctantly, Celia had to admit she'd never seen a more handsome or seductive man. Luckily, her temper helped her keep her distance.

She'd already had enough bad luck with men, almost marrying one who quite possibly intended to murder her for her money. She had no intention of falling for the strange recluse Cameron Alexander, even if he was the most intriguing man she'd ever met.

He took most of the day to put the sailboat to rights, and she was relieved to escape the islet as hordes of mosquitoes and midges descended for an evening feast. Her resolve and anger, which she had stoked all afternoon, wavered when he carried her in his arms to the righted sailboat. The warmth and closeness of him took her breath away.

Once in the boat, she distracted herself from Cameron's proximity by studying the skiff that he was tying to the back of the sailboat. A canvas sail furled around a makeshift mast in the boat's center and a rough rudder on the floor of the boat explained how Cameron had managed to catch up with her so quickly. Only the most adept sailor, however, could have survived the recent storm in such a craft. Cameron was evidently world-class.

As he climbed aboard, she hunkered down with her back toward him, afraid to face him until she could gather her whirling thoughts and tamp down her unwanted attraction to him. They were returning to Solitaire, she reminded herself, her prison for the next twelve weeks.

If not forever.

Once the sails had filled and the boat skimmed swiftly along the open water, she braced herself for a torrent of angry words and accusations at her escape attempt, but Cameron remained as silent and unfathomable as the water's depths.

Unwilling to meet his eyes, she studied the gathering darkness along the shore, the gentle wave action of the gulf, the smudged pastel palette of the fading sunset on the clouds—anything to avoid the self-satisfied expression of the man at the tiller.

Above, the high, thin cry of the curved-beak curlew sounded as the flocks made their way to their inland rookeries for the night. Cameron shifted his gaze to watch their flight, then looked away quickly when his glance fell upon her once more. He rolled his neck and shoulders, and she realized how they must ache from hours of fighting the makeshift tiller of the skiff against the storm, then hours more refloating his sailboat.

Her skin burned from extended exposure to the sun and wind, and her eyes watered from the hours of glaring sunlight bouncing off the water, and she wondered if Cameron was as uncomfortable.

She stared into the wide stretches of empty, open water, yearning for the appearance of a Jet Ski, windsurfer, or a cabin cruiser filled with tourists, anyone who might rescue her from Cameron and return her home. But the sailboat and the skiff towed behind it were the only vessels visible on the endless waters of the gulf.

They had been sailing for almost an hour before she finally gathered courage to speak. If she had to remain with him, she needed to keep their interaction on polite terms. She called to Cameron above the snapping sails and splashing water. ''I haven't thanked you for coming after me. I'm grateful.''

Her words weren't a lie. Just as surely as his refusal to help her had driven her into the wilderness, he alone had rescued her from almost certain death from exposure.

He stared at her with his strange amber eyes, and

in the failing light, she couldn't tell what emotion, if any, lurked behind them. "No need to thank me. It's my fault, after all."

She nodded in agreement. What he'd said was true enough. She turned her attention to the shoreline again, all of it monotonously the same, towering mangroves giving way inland to tangled woodlands, saw palmettos and cabbage palms, a scene that remained constant as the boat drank up the miles. The solitude surged toward her, as if to draw her into its depths once more.

She turned to Cameron to stave off the loneliness. "How did you find me? I counted on your heading south for Key West."

The wind had dropped, the snapping canvas had quieted, and she no longer had to shout to be heard over the curling water.

He hooked the tiller beneath his arm and rummaged in his shirt pocket, extracting a pipe and tobacco pouch. "Yesterday morning, I was in my study, bringing my journals up to date, a task I'd never neglected until you washed up on my beach."

She didn't know whether to feel flattered or to apologize, but feared if she interrupted him, he'd retreat into silence again. After he'd tamped fragrant tobacco into the bowl of his pipe with his thumb, then put a match to it, he held the tiller in one hand, his pipe in the other, and continued his story. He related how Mrs. Givens had spotted Celia's departure and alerted Cameron, how he and Noah had outfitted the skiff with sail, and how he'd set off at once to overtake her.

"All the while," he said, "I feared you had too great a lead, that I would never catch you."

She shuddered at his words. The man was unswerving in his determination never to let her leave.

She tried again to read his face, but darkness had set in, and she could only wonder whether concern for her safety or for the return of his boat and the safeguarding of his hideaway had driven Cameron so relentlessly in his pursuit of her.

The blackness of the night closed in around them, broken only by the faint light of the waning moon, myriad brilliant stars and a green phosphorescence dancing on the water. The barking cough of a panther punctuated the stillness of the dark maze of wilderness directly to the east. From another part of the glades came the guttural snarl of a bobcat. Celia shivered again, wondering what might have happened to her if Cameron hadn't found her.

"It was already storming when I reached this area last night," Cameron said, "and I almost gave up hope."

He muttered something so soft and low she barely heard it, but his whispered words made the hair stand up on the back of her neck. "If you had died, I would have another death on my conscience."

Another death?

Who had died, and why did Cameron feel responsible? Her curiosity burned, but she kept her questions to herself.

The wind freshened, carrying a hint of autumn in the dry air. Exposed to the cool night air, her skin broke out in goose bumps, and her teeth began to chatter as the chill seeped into her bones. She thought longingly of hot coffee.

"Miss Stevens."

She had drawn herself into a ball to stay warm, and when she lifted her head at his call, Cameron beckoned her to sit beside him. By then, she was so miserably cold, she'd have sat by the devil himself to stay warm. She climbed back to where Cameron sat in the stern, and he pulled her next to him, wrapping his free arm around her while the other guided the boat.

"Better?" he asked.

She nodded, then laid her head against his chest to maximize the warmth his body offered. She couldn't avoid inhaling the scent of sunshine, salt spray and the pleasant masculine musk of the man himself. Beneath the hard muscles of his chest, his heart thudded against her ear. Above, the sails cracked, reflecting the colors of the night.

"'Purple the sails, and so perfumed, that the winds were lovesick with them.'" The words from Shakespeare sprang automatically to her lips.

"*Antony and Cleopatra?*" Cameron asked.

"Yes."

"You like literature?"

"I love books. That's why I bought a bookstore."

"I'm fond of books myself," he admitted.

"Let's make a game," she suggested. "One of us

quotes a line about ships or sailing and the other has
to guess the title or the author.''

The nearness of the man had stirred dangerous
emotions best ignored, so she had proposed the game
as a diversion.

''My turn, then.'' He thought for a moment. '''But
in a sieve I'll thither sail, and, like a rat without a
tail—'''

''That's too easy. *Macbeth.* But one easy one de-
serves another. 'And all I ask is a tall ship and a star
to steer her by.'''

''Sea Fever,'' he answered instantly, ''by John
Masefield.''

She'd had her ship, she'd tried her escape and she'd
failed. In spite of the attractiveness of her captor, she
was still a prisoner. Frustrated by her lack of freedom,
exhausted by her ordeal, she couldn't contain a deep,
choking sob.

Cameron tightened his hold as she cried herself to
sleep against the broad width of his chest. She roused
only once during the long night—or maybe she'd simply dreamed—when Cameron brushed the hair from
her forehead and pressed his lips there.

''Celia Stevens.'' He had uttered her name like a
long sigh. ''What have you done to me? And what
am I to do with you?''

WHEN CELIA AWOKE LATE IN the afternoon of the day
of their return to Solitaire, her twelve weeks on the
island stretched before her like an eternity and the
questions that had plagued her since her arrival

swarmed like no-see-ums. Why had Cameron hidden himself away on the island? Was he an outcast? A fugitive from justice?

She shook away such thoughts. Except for his insistence on keeping her prisoner—or, as he asserted, a guest—and his brief spurt of anger when she'd lighted her signal fire, Cameron didn't seem dangerous. His actions toward her had been both courteous and kind. Mrs. Givens had hinted that he suffered from a sickness of the spirit, but Celia couldn't picture Cameron as mentally ill.

She sighed and pushed the disturbing thoughts away. She would have plenty of time to learn more about Cameron and his island hideaway. Delving into his secrets would give her something to do for the next three months. Resigned for the moment to her captivity, she dressed and went downstairs to find Mrs. Givens in the front room, polishing furniture.

The housekeeper pushed a gray curl off her forehead and smiled. "Ah, the slugabed has arisen. I left something for you on the kitchen table. It should hold you until dinner."

Glad Mrs. Givens hadn't chastised her for her unsuccessful escape attempt, Celia thanked her and continued through the house to the kitchen. Considering the wilderness Celia had plunged into of her own accord, the housekeeper probably doubted Celia's sanity.

Mrs. Givens hadn't been awake earlier that morning when Celia and Cameron had docked the sailboat in the early dawn.

"Do not attempt to leave here again," he'd warned as they walked through the sea mist toward the house.

Celia couldn't tell if his words held the tenor of a threat or a plea. He'd left her then, and she hadn't seen him since. She'd stumbled upstairs to bed and fallen asleep fully clothed. When she'd awakened a few moments ago, she'd washed away the sand in the basin in her room and donned the borrowed garments from Mrs. Givens, leaving her saltwater and sand-filled clothes to launder later.

In the kitchen, as Mrs. Givens had promised, Celia found a napkin-covered plate that held fluffy biscuits filled with thin slivers of ham and slices of fresh pineapple. She took one and wandered down the kitchen steps, hoping to find Cameron, but her host had disappeared.

Noah was in the vegetable garden chopping weeds with a hoe.

"Want some help?" she asked.

He looked up in surprise, then leaned one arm on his hoe while he wiped his face with his sleeve.

"No, ma'am. It's hot and dirty work for a lady. But I sure would like somebody to talk to. Makes the work go faster."

She settled onto a large stump nearby, guessing from the grooves in its surface it was used for chopping kindling, and nibbled her belated breakfast.

"How long have you worked for Mr. Alexander?" she asked.

"Ever since we came here, six years ago."

"Did you come with him from England?"

Her question was more than idle conversation. Celia hoped Noah would shed some light on the reason Cameron had left his native land. Her interest grew not only out of concern for her safety but also out of the strange effect Cameron had on her. He'd become her last thought before sleeping, her first fancy on waking and the person she looked for when she entered a room.

Noah, not realizing her motives, told her about himself. "I met Mr. Alex in Key West. I come from South Carolina, but I'd been working on a shrimp boat out of the keys."

"Why did you come here?"

Noah's dark eyes clouded. "They was a fight on the boat. One man gutted another with a fish knife. I had nothing to do with it, but the crew decided they'd put the blame on me. When we reached port and they called the cops, I ran. Hid on Captain Biggins's boat. That's where I met Mr. Alex."

"And that's why you can't leave here?"

He nodded sadly. "If the police catch me, it's my word against three others. I don't want to go to jail. I'd shrivel up and die if I couldn't be outdoors."

Her appetite disappeared at Noah's story. She crumbled the remainder of her biscuit and scattered it for the gulls.

"Living on this island isn't my idea of freedom," she said.

"Where was I gonna hide? And how was I gonna earn a living? When I told him my story, Mr. Alex asked me if I'd come work for him, and I said yes. We came to this island that same day.''

She glanced around at the garden and the wood pile, both Noah's domain. ''You work hard, don't you?''

A broad grin split his face. ''I don't mind working hard. When we first came, Mr. Alex worked as long and hard as me to build this house. Even now he works, too, hunting and fishing for food, chopping wood when need be. He's a good man, Mr. Alex is.''

Pondering Cameron's goodness with more than a pinch of doubt, she gazed across the dunes rising between her and the gulf.

''But I ain't told you the best part,'' Noah said. ''Every week since I came here, Mr. Alex gives me my pay. I been saving it up for when I'm too old and feeble to work. That's when I'll leave here and go to Canada or maybe even to Africa, where the Key West law can't find me. I'm a lucky man.''

He was lucky to have avoided being arrested, falsely accused and imprisoned, but beneath his surface cheerfulness, Celia sensed a deep sadness. He had to be lonely, in spite of his gratitude at being free.

For Mrs. Givens and Noah, their work took all their time, especially without the modern conveniences that Celia was accustomed to, but how Cameron spent his days remained a mystery.

''How does Mr. Alexander pass his time?'' she asked.

''He studies things.''

"Books?"

"Sometimes books. He's got stacks of 'em in his study and Captain Biggins is always bringing more. But mostly Mr. Alex studies plants and flowers and fish and animals."

"Is he a scientist? A naturalist?"

Noah shrugged. "I think he just likes 'em. And he leaves things where he finds 'em. He don't hold with cages or killing things for—" He scratched his head. "What was that word?"

"Specimens?"

"Yeah, that's it. He believes what the Good Book says, that people should be stewards of the earth."

"He's right, Noah." She stood and shook her cumbersome skirt. "If we don't take care of the earth, a hundred years from now, this could all be ruined."

Noah threw back his head and laughed. "You're joshing, Miss Celia. All this land and water? Why, it's enough to last to the end of time."

That's what too many people thought, she grumbled to herself as she walked back to the house.

Her conversation with Noah had taught her more about Cameron, revealing his positive traits to add to the less stellar ones he had exhibited since her arrival. He also had a treasure she was anxious to share. A study full of books.

Mrs. Givens was singing in the kitchen as she prepared dinner, and Cameron was nowhere in sight when Celia entered the house.

She slipped into his study to search for something to read and closed the door behind her. Through the open French doors of the room, she could view the path to the beach, but Cameron wasn't in sight.

The walls of bookcases overflowed with volumes, and stacks of books littered the floor. A wing chair and ottoman, upholstered in maroon leather and flanked by a campaign chest holding a decanter of whiskey and glasses, stood within arm's reach of the shelves. Cameron's frame was imprinted in the chair's leather cushions, and she sat, molding her body to the impressions in the leather, thinking disturbingly intimate thoughts of the man who'd made those indentations.

Disconcerted by the direction her thoughts were taking, she scrambled to her feet and returned her attention to the shelves. Her survey revealed books on meteorology, astronomy, ornithology, botany, horticulture and zoology. On the opposite wall were Shakespeare's plays, several slim volumes of poetry, classical novels and dozens of the past year's bestsellers. She studied the titles, but they told her nothing about Cameron except that his taste in reading was eclectic.

Consumed by curiosity to know more about the man who held her hostage and who haunted her waking dreams, she was drawn to his desk, a large mahogany structure that dominated the room. She settled into the chair behind it and inspected the pipe rack, humidor and pens and pencils on its polished surface. Neatly piled to one side were several bound journals. With only a slight twinge of conscience over her snooping, she opened the top one. Written in a bold, clear hand were the day's date and a summary of the weather and tides of the previous day. A peek at the other journals revealed records of bird sightings, fish catches and plant and wildlife observations.

What little she had learned from Noah about Cameron had only whetted her appetite for more. She slid open the top right drawer of his desk. Stacked inside were folders filled with papers. The top folder held bills and receipts for supplies, but the second, filled with old newspaper articles, proved more interesting. She picked it up and a yellowed clipping fluttered to the floor.

Celia retrieved the clipping, an article from the London *Times* dated over seven years earlier. The headline read Heiress And Son Murdered, Killer At Large.

Intrigued, Celia read further:

Yesterday police discovered the bodies of Clarissa Wingate Alexander, heir to the Wingate mining empire, and her son, Randolph, in their country estate on the Devon coast. Although authorities have released no specifics, the pair were brutally murdered. Police have no suspects in the killings, and Cameron Alexander, the bereaved husband and father—

At the sound of footsteps on the veranda outside the study, Celia stuffed the clipping back into the folder, jammed the folder in the drawer and slammed it shut. She scampered across the room to the shelves of novels, grabbed the handiest book, and opened it, pretending to read.

She looked up to find Cameron, leaning against the door frame and watching her. With the sunlight behind him, his face was unreadable in the shadows, but the irritation in his voice was unmistakable.

"Did you find what you were looking for?"

Chapter Five

Cameron stepped into his study and confronted Celia, who stood at the bookcase across the room like a child who'd been caught with her hand in the biscuit tin. She had obviously been snooping, but what, if anything, had she discovered? The flush on her face could have been embarrassment, distress, or merely the sunburn she'd suffered from yesterday's escape attempt.

Before he could speak, she glanced at the book she held in her hands, discovered it was upside-down, and righted it quickly.

Cameron repressed a grin. God, the woman had spunk. He'd caught her red-handed rifling through his office, but she'd recovered her composure and faced him now, head high, chin out, eyes blazing with innocence. She was absolutely fearless, a woman who had braved the unknown in a strange boat within days of a terrible shipwreck that almost killed her. Her courage evoked a tenderness toward her that he fought to repress. For now, he had to avoid this woman who held such fascination for him.

"I was looking for something to read," she said in a clear, unwavering tone and held the volume out to him.

He moved closer, careful to keep his suspicions and his attraction hidden. He glanced at the title and raised an eyebrow. "*Paradise Lost.* An interesting choice."

"I hope you don't mind." Her straightforward gaze challenged him.

Only with the strongest resolve did he hold himself in check, when what he wanted most was to take the book from her and draw her to him, to feel the softness of her skin against his— He yanked his rebellious thoughts back in line. "On the contrary. Help yourself to any book you wish. They make good company."

With a nonchalance he didn't feel with his senses stirring at his proximity to her, so close he could inhale the delightful frangipani-scented soap she'd bathed with, he moved across the room. With studied casualness, he took a small key from the top of his desk and locked the drawers. He would share their contents someday with his uninvited guest, but not yet. First, he had to win her trust and her loyalty.

"I hope you haven't suffered ill effects from your recent trip." He placed the key in the pocket of his shirt and resisted the tender feelings welling in him, generated by her bravado at being caught snooping. Celia Stevens was an intelligent woman. She would demand answers to why she was being held prisoner and persist until she'd ferreted out the reason for her captivity. But he must make her wait as long as possible before knowing the truth.

For both their sakes.

She shook her head. "No ill effects. Just a touch of sunburn."

Longing to remain in her company, but afraid to trust his reactions to his beautiful guest, he turned toward the door. "Take any book you want," he repeated and rushed headlong toward the beach and solitude.

He had questions of his own he wanted answered. Why had Celia been wearing a wedding gown when he and Noah had first discovered her cast up on his beach? Had she been running from—or to—marriage? And why should her marital state matter to him?

SHAKEN, CELIA WATCHED him go. With the knowledge the newspaper clipping had given her, she viewed Cameron from a new perspective, understanding at last why he'd chosen to withdraw to the privacy of his island in the Florida wilderness. To have lost both his wife and child in such a violent manner must have devastated him. No wonder Mrs. Givens wouldn't speak of it. Any references or remembrances would only bring him more pain.

The desire to follow Cameron, to place her arms around him and console him swept through her, until she realized that her stoic host didn't look as if he'd be easily comforted. Then another thought struck her.

If Cameron had simply withdrawn in grief, why the obsessive need to keep his whereabouts secret?

She'd do well to stay as far away as possible from her attractive captor until she had answered that question to her satisfaction.

For the next few days, she saw little of Cameron. Her time was spent with Mrs. Givens, who had recruited Celia into a campaign to provide her with a proper wardrobe.

After breakfast each morning, they cleared the large kitchen table and spread out fabrics for cutting. Mrs. Givens contributed several lengths of cotton cloth, one a leaf green, another a deep blue, and the third a pale yellow. Celia knew the materials had been intended for the housekeeper's own use, but Mrs. Givens brushed aside her protests.

"We'll make you some casual clothes, but you should have a few dresses, too." The housekeeper gazed at the ill-fitting borrowed clothes Celia was wearing. "Even in the wilderness, we try to keep our ways civilized."

Doubting the usefulness of dresses, but acknowledging that she would soon wear out her one pair of shorts and only shirt, Celia applied herself diligently with needle and thread. To her surprise, she found she could produce a small, neat stitch and she began to enjoy sewing.

Mrs. Givens, after measuring every circumference and length of Celia, cut underclothes from fine linen sheets, and Celia stitched them while the housekeeper constructed patterns for dresses, shorts and shirts.

The sewing times created an oasis of camaraderie and happiness in the long, lonely days as Celia waited for the time to pass. The hot, humid weather had broken the day of her return from her escape attempt, and mornings in the kitchen, even with the cooking fire blazing in the wood stove, were comfortable and pleasant with the French doors open to the sea breeze.

The enticing aromas of baking always filled the room, from the yeasty tang of dinner rolls to the spicy scent of gingerbread. A true Englishwoman, Mrs. Givens kept the kettle boiling and constantly replenished the teacup at Celia's elbow. Had Celia not been homesick and concerned over her eventual fate, plus struggling to understand her inexplicable longing to spend more time with her elusive host, she would have found even greater satisfaction in those hours of tranquil domesticity.

Mrs. Givens chattered as she worked, telling stories of her childhood in Liverpool, of Mr. Givens's death at sea some thirty-five years earlier, and of Cameron's childhood. "I went to work for the Alexanders right after my Arthur died. Mr. Alexander—Cameron—had just been born, and his mother wasn't well, so the child needed me. And I needed him, broken up as I was over losing my Arthur."

"And you've been with him all this time?"

"Aye, I raised him from a babe, then took over the housekeeping for him and his father when his poor mother and baby brother died in childbirth. Cameron was only four years old."

"Is his father still alive?"

"Died when the lad was fifteen. Thrown from a horse and broke his neck. That loss almost killed Cameron."

"They were close?"

"He worshiped his father. Went quite wild after Mr. Alexander died. I'd hoped Clarissa—"

Mrs. Givens clamped her jaw shut, got up and took the kettle off the stove. She busied herself refilling the teapot, avoiding Celia's gaze.

"Is that Clarissa's portrait in the front room?" Celia asked.

Mrs. Givens returned the kettle to the stove, crossed to the open doorway overlooking the bay, and gazed toward the pier as if to assure herself that Cameron's sloop was still gone. She returned and settled herself into her rocker by the fire. "You must never speak her name in this house."

"Why?" Celia couldn't admit that she understood. She was ashamed to confess to snooping in Cameron's desk.

"It's too painful for Mr. Alexander."

"She's dead?"

Mrs. Givens nodded and tears filled her eyes. "And little Randolph, too. I'd raised him from a baby, just like his father."

"I'm sorry."

"It was horrible, just horrible." The housekeeper's lips trembled and tears flowed down her cheeks.

Celia poured her a fresh cup of tea, added milk and sugar the way Mrs. Givens liked it, and handed her the cup. "I shouldn't have mentioned…I didn't mean to upset you."

Mrs. Givens took a noisy sip of tea, set the cup aside, and blew her nose loudly on a lace-trimmed handkerchief. "I'm all right, luv. Days go by without my thinking of them at all, and then suddenly, out of the blue, I remember, and it's as if it just happened."

"I can understand why you don't want anything said around Mr. Alexander. It must be awful for him, too."

Mrs. Givens snapped up her head and drilled Celia with a penetrating stare. "What do you know about it?"

"Nothing." She couldn't help blushing at her lie. "Only what you've told me."

"Then let it go at that. Their deaths were a terrible, terrible…accident, and it's best we don't speak of them again."

Accident?

Celia longed to ask the housekeeper more, but speaking of it upset Mrs. Givens so much, Celia knew she would be cruel to press the issue. Maybe the housekeeper thought the word *murder* so sinister, she couldn't bring herself to use it.

Celia returned to her sewing, and Mrs. Givens did the same, putting the finishing touches on the deep blue dress, a slender sleeveless sheath with a scooped neck that would be cool and comfortable in the Florida weather, but where Celia would wear it was a puzzle. All she needed were shorts and shirts. Aside from walking the beach, she spent her time either in the kitchen or reading in her room. She didn't require a dress for any of those activities.

And she certainly didn't need a new dress to please her elusive host. That day, as had been his custom since her arrival, Cameron took his lunch in a basket on his sloop, where he spent most of the day. He ate dinner either alone in his study or in the formal dining room, but Mrs. Givens served Celia's dinner with hers in the kitchen or carried it up to her room on a tray.

Cameron continued to evade Celia, and she wondered if he had seen her going through his desk and was avoiding her as a way of showing his disapproval.

While Mrs. Givens's companionship was pleasant, Celia missed her home and friends. She missed the bustle of customers in her bookstore, the friendly chatter, book discussions and innocuous gossip that had filled her days. She missed her house on the beach and the familiar routine of her life. And always, like a dull persistent pain, she grieved for her parents who had died too young in a car crash. More than anything, she wanted to leave this island and go home.

The only thing she didn't miss was Darren Walker.

She had fallen in love disastrously, she realized now. She'd been too dazed by her parents' recent deaths, too anxious for someone to lean on to have chosen wisely. That bad decision was all the more reason for her to rein in her attraction to Cameron. And all the more reason for her to leave Solitaire as soon as possible. But when Cameron or Noah wasn't using the sailboat or skiff, the crafts were chained and padlocked to the docks. She had no means of escape.

Her days fell into a pattern. She'd rise early, although never early enough again to catch Cameron in his morning swim. He'd always had breakfast and left the house by the time Celia joined Mrs. Givens in the kitchen. After breakfast, Celia sewed until lunchtime. After lunch, she walked the beach, collecting shells and watching countless seabirds. Sometimes, if both Cameron and Noah were away from the island, she would strip off her clothes and swim in the warm, clear waters until she was so tired that she slept afterward in the shade of a dune.

Once during such a swim, Celia looked back toward the house and thought she saw Cameron watching from the second-floor veranda. She dove beneath the water, and when she surfaced and looked again, he was gone. She wondered then if she'd really seen him or if her own preoccupation with him had created the illusion.

Nighttime was the hardest, when homesickness and loneliness seared through her. To pass the interminable hours between dinner and sleep, she worked her way through the books in Cameron's study, sometimes completing a book a night.

A week after Celia's unsuccessful escape attempt, a cold front brought a day of drizzling rain. There was nothing to prevent her from walking in the soft downpour, but her spirits flagged at the gray weather, and she stayed indoors, wandering listlessly through the big house. She tried to read but couldn't concentrate, tried to sleep but couldn't, and finally joined Mrs. Givens in the kitchen.

"There you are." The housekeeper greeted her with a warm smile. "Come have a cup of tea."

Mrs. Givens put her sewing aside and began setting out the tea service. "Your blue dress is finished, and tomorrow I can start on the yellow one. It's a lovely change to sew for such a trim figure."

She smoothed her apron over her ample curves and sliced generous wedges from a huge cake.

Celia reached for the plate Mrs. Givens offered, and, without warning, a bolt of lightning struck the beach not a hundred feet from the kitchen. It blasted the fronds from a cabbage palm and filled the air with the acrid scent of ozone and burning branches. The greenish glow of its fire called up unwanted memories of the horrific storm that had destroyed Celia's sailboat and tossed her onto Cameron's beach. Remembering the trauma, she felt her heart begin to hammer, her chest tighten and the room spin.

"Here, what's this?" she heard Mrs. Givens say through the gathering blackness.

The plate of cake dropped from Celia's hand and shattered on the floor. She lay her head on the table, struggling for air, fighting against the panic attack that threatened to consume her.

Mrs. Givens's plump fingers probed at her wrist, assessing her pulse, and her other hand clasped Celia's forehead. "You have no fever, m'dear, but your pulse is pounding like a drum."

Celia was only vaguely aware of Mrs. Givens's

dress rustling as she moved across the kitchen. Over the thundering of blood in her ears, she heard a stopper pulled from a bottle and a splashing of liquid.

"Here, luv, take a deep sip of this." Mrs. Givens pulled her upright and held a cup to her lips.

Celia swallowed a mouthful of the bitter tea.

"Now, a little more. Drink it all down. That's my girl." The housekeeper set the cup aside, pulled a chair next to Celia and sat with her arm around her shoulders, patting her reassuringly all the while.

The panic attack held Celia firmly in its grip. She was hyperventilating. She pushed back from the table and Mrs. Givens's grasp and lowered her head between her knees, trying to will the dizziness away.

Mrs. Givens kept a firm grip on her shoulders. "You're just having a spell of nerves, and no wonder, after all you've been through. Shipwrecked twice and marooned with strangers."

Celia tried to assure her that she'd be all right, but she couldn't gather enough breath to speak.

"I've given you a bit of my herb remedy to calm you," the housekeeper said. "You'll feel it working soon, but before it does, we'd better get you up to bed."

Celia tried to stand, but her legs gave way.

"What's going on?" Cameron's rich voice rolled through the kitchen, but Celia couldn't force her eyes open to look at him.

Suddenly, she found herself once again gathered in his arms, her cheek pressed against his chest, the appealing male scent of him filling her nostrils, the thud of his heartbeat a comforting rhythm in her ears. Her panic eased, but whether from Mrs. Givens's remedy or Cameron's reassuring embrace, she couldn't tell.

As if she weighed nothing, he carried her upstairs and laid her on her bed. His hands were gentle as he removed her shoes and spread a comforter over her. She was slipping into a drugged sleep when she heard him leave.

From the room next door floated Mrs. Givens's voice, raised in anger. "Cameron Alexander, that poor young thing is not only bored but frightened to death."

"What do you expect me to do about it?" His flat tone betrayed no feeling.

"Ah!" Frustration sharpened the housekeeper's voice. "Sometimes I despair of you, I really do!"

"Calm yourself, Mrs. Givens, and say what you mean."

"If you insist on keeping that poor girl here, you must treat her more kindly, or I'll go for the authorities myself, and *then* where will you be?"

Celia struggled to comprehend the curious exchange and listened for Cameron's answer, but she couldn't stay awake. She fell into a deep sleep and didn't know if she dreamed or actually awakened in the night to the dark figure of a man at the foot of her bed, outlined against the moonlight shining through the French doors, watching her until she lost consciousness again.

CELIA SLEPT THROUGH the night and into the next morning, convinced when she awoke that she had dreamed the figure at the foot of her bed. Cameron, after all, wanted nothing more than his solitude, and the only time she'd seen Noah recently, who had his own little cottage near the garden, in the house was the day he'd carried in the copper tub for her bath.

Both her depression and her terror from the day before had vanished, and the only remnant of her ordeal was a mouth lined with cotton, a side effect of Mrs. Givens's "remedy." She dressed quickly and hurried down to the kitchen for something to wash the woolliness away.

Mrs. Givens greeted her with all the enthusiasm of a songbird at sunrise. She took a flat iron from the woodstove, tested its heat with a wet finger, and began pressing the hem of Celia's new blue dress. "Feeling better, are we?"

"Only terribly thirsty." Celia poured a glass of water and drank it down.

"That's the one bad thing about my cure for anxiety, but you'll be fine now." The housekeeper pointed to an open shelf above an antique pie safe. "Those are all my special herbal remedies. Learned them from my grandmother."

Celia considered the bottles and jars of strange liquids, dried powders and herbs and was glad she was young and healthy. Those folk remedies were the closest she'd come to a doctor or pharmacy in the wilderness. "I've never had such an attack before and hope never to again."

"Time will heal." Mrs. Givens replaced the flat

iron on the stove, shook out the blue dress, and laid it carefully across a chair. "This will be perfect for you to wear tonight."

"Tonight?"

"Mr. Alexander had decided to hold a celebration in honor of your visit here. I'm preparing a special dinner, so there'll be no sewing time today."

Celia left the housekeeper flurrying in the kitchen, seemingly as excited as if the queen were coming to dine. She couldn't help wondering over the shift in Cameron's attitude and whether Mrs. Givens's threats of alerting the authorities or a change of heart had precipitated it.

Taking Cameron's copy of *Rebecca* and feeling like a character in a gothic novel herself, she walked down to the beach. Finding a puddle of shade beneath one of the dunes, she settled down to read, but her mind wandered from the pages to the predicament that trapped her.

Almost two weeks ago she had washed ashore on Solitaire, and in about ten more weeks Captain Biggins would arrive to take her away. With both Cameron's boats inaccessible, she had no means of escape until then. She could rail against her situation all she wanted, but her protests would change nothing. Perhaps the time would pass more quickly if she treated her imprisonment as a holiday. The setting was certainly one most vacationers would envy. Both Mrs. Givens and Noah had befriended her and were doing all they could to make her feel at home.

She drew lazy circles in the sand with the tip of a

finger and reluctantly admitted that the greatest attraction on the island was Cameron Alexander, her mysterious host. She recalled his kindness when he had rescued her from the mangrove island and the pressure of his lips against her forehead when he thought her asleep on the voyage home. In spite of his reclusive nature and expressed desire to be left alone, she sensed in him the same needs as her own, the longing for love and companionship. She was still smarting too much from Darren's deception to consider loving again, but she hoped that during the coming weeks, she and Cameron could at least be friends.

"Good morning, Miss Stevens."

She hadn't heard Cameron approach in the soft sand and started at the sound of his voice.

He knelt beside her, his eyes hidden by the broad brim of his hat. "Are you recovered from yesterday?"

Embarrassed by her panic attack, she nodded her head. "I'm fine, thanks."

"I've been remiss in my duties as a host." He stared out to sea and broke off a spray of sea oats, shredding the kernels from the stem.

"You've been very hospitable—"

"Not as I should have been, but I intend to make that up to you now. Mrs. Givens tells me you have a new dress." He turned to face her, his eyes glowing with a strange heat, his mouth lifted in an irresistible smile. "Will you wear it for me tonight?"

Her pulse raced at his expression, and she reminded herself of her earlier declaration of friendship and no

more. Without success, she tried to read between the
lines, to understand why, after ignoring her for so
long, he had finally decided to recognize her existence
on his island.

"Join me on the west veranda at sunset for drinks.
Then Mrs. Givens will serve us a feast." He settled
back on his heels, pushed the brim of his hat back
with one finger, and turned the full radiance of his
smile on her.

She felt the caress of the gulf breeze on her cheek,
heard the cry of a curlew above her, and saw kneeling
before her the most exciting man she'd ever met. She
wanted to imprint the scene on her senses so that in
the years ahead, she could call it up and reexperience
the perfection of the moment.

"I'd be delighted," she said.

He acknowledged her acceptance with a nod, stood
and walked away.

NOAH CARRIED THE COPPER tub and gallons of hot
water up to Celia's room in the late afternoon, and
she soaked happily in the bath before washing her
hair with Mrs. Givens's homemade soap. Her new
dress lay across the bed, and she felt a crescendo of
excitement, like a teenager preparing for a prom.

She tried to convince herself that her anticipation
was due solely to the prospect of a new experience,
something to break the routine of her captivity, but
she couldn't deny the warmth she'd noted in Cameron's eyes when he'd issued his invitation and the
corresponding flutter in her heart.

She was just donning her underclothes when Mrs. Givens poked her head into the room. "I want to see how your dress looks."

Celia slipped the dress over her head. It settled with a perfect fit into an A-line that skimmed her breasts and hips and stopped just above her knees. She pirouetted to give the housekeeper a full view. "It's a lovely dress, and you're a wonderful seamstress. Thank you, Mrs. Givens."

Mrs. Givens clasped her hands in approval. "You're absolutely radiant, m'dear. A delight for any man's eyes."

Celia caught the matchmaking gleam in the housekeeper's expression and wondered about the woman's motives for attempting to turn the ugly duckling castaway onto their island into a swan.

"There's a full-length mirror in the room across the hall," Mrs. Givens said. "Have a look at yourself. You've come a long way from the day you washed onto our beach."

Celia crossed the hall and considered her image in the tall glass. Her scrapes and bruises from the initial shipwreck had healed, the welts from insect bites during her escape attempt had disappeared, and the woman who looked back at her was slender and golden-tan with sun-streaked hair, all an agreeable contrast to the deep blue fabric of her dress. She had only her old sneakers as shoes, but they would have to do, and she hoped her appearance would be pleasing enough to continue the thaw in Cameron's demeanor.

She wasn't disappointed at the impression she made. When she approached him on the western veranda as the sun was sinking toward the horizon, he looked as if he couldn't believe his eyes.

"Miss Stevens, you look lovely."

Not only had Cameron thawed, the look he gave her threatened to melt her where she stood. When he handed her a spray of wild and delicate butterfly orchids, their white petals tinged with purple, she was happy for the loose bodice of her dress, because she was having trouble breathing.

Cameron had also taken pains with his clothes. He wore a collarless white shirt topped with a leather vest and fitted pants tucked into gleaming riding boots. The clothes accented the broadness of his shoulders, and the power of his thighs, calling back to memory the sight of his naked form diving into the waves.

Celia was no prude, but the memory—with Cameron in the flesh before her—made her blush. She attempted to steer her thoughts and the conversation to safer ground. "May I ask a favor?"

Beside Cameron, a small table covered with a linen cloth held a decanter and glasses. He poured a glass of the white wine and handed it to her. "Anything, Miss Stevens."

"Would you call me Celia? I'm not used to such formality. It's not our custom here in the States."

"When in Rome…" He raised his glass in a salute. "To Celia, health and happiness."

She raised her glass in return and sipped the dry wine, wishing nostalgically for a glass of chilled chardonnay. Only the British, she thought wryly, could survive in a tropical country without ice.

"Cameron," he said.

"What?"

"If we're to observe your American custom, you must call me Cameron."

"Thank you—Cameron."

"Come. It's almost time. We must watch."

"Watch what?"

He pointed to the setting sun. Such was the easy pace of life on Solitaire that the high point of the day was the spectacle of sunset. They leaned against the balustrade, following the course of the fiery disc as it dropped behind a thin veil of clouds before plunging into the gulf waters turned molten gold by its light.

As the last sliver disappeared, she felt Cameron tense beside her.

"Not this time." He sighed and tossed back the remainder of his wine.

She threw him a questioning glance, and he pulled two rustic chairs, fashioned from bamboo with woven seats, up to the railing. She took one chair and Cameron sat beside her and pulled his chair closer.

"The first month I was on this island," he said, "I witnessed a strange phenomenon. It had rained that afternoon, and the storm clouds passed over and out into the gulf. At sunset, only a strip of sky was visible between the sea and the underside of the clouds."

"That happens all the time." She couldn't understand why he seemed so animated over an ordinary sunset.

"Not what I saw that night. I've watched the sunset every evening since then, over two thousand nights, and I have never seen it again. It was amazing."

He leaned forward, rolling the wineglass between his palms. His eyes sparkled with an enthusiasm Celia hadn't seen there before.

"That evening," he continued, "the instant the sun disappeared below the horizon, there was a magnificent flash of green, as if the sun had been dropped from a great height into a lake of green light that splashed upward like a fountain."

"*A Flash of Green*—shades of John D. McDonald." She visualized the classic mystery by that title in its place on the shelf in Sand Castles.

"McDonald?"

"One of Florida's best mystery writers. He wrote a book titled *A Flash of Green*."

"I must order it when Captain Biggins comes again."

"I can send it to you from my bookstore when I return," she offered.

The look he gave her was unfathomable, making her wonder what the man was thinking. How could she trust his motives when she didn't even know what they were?

"I watch every night," he said, making her uneasy about her eventual release by not commenting on her offer, "hoping to see the light again, but it continues to elude me."

"I've watched for it, too, but never witnessed it.

I've read somewhere you have a one in a million chance of seeing it. Maybe you'll never see it again.''

"You could be right. I suppose I will have to satisfy myself with the bizarre green lights I have seen in the sky lately in the dead of night.''

"Green lights? I never heard of such a thing, except for St. Elmo's fire.'' A memory of that greenish glow racing along the rigging of her sailboat before it capsized sent a chill down her spine. She pushed the disturbing thought away, afraid of precipitating another panic attack.

"Think of the horizon as the boom of a ship,'' he said, as if he'd read her mind, "and those huge cumulus clouds that we see with summer storms as St. Elmo's fire. That is what I saw in the gulf the night before we found you on the beach.''

Cameron had witnessed the storm that had ripped her from her boat and thrown her onto the sands of Solitaire. The thought brought back to her with a vengeance her status as prisoner on the island. But if she had to be a captive, she would make the best of it—and the best sat beside her in the seductive form of Cameron Alexander.

Chapter Six

Celia sat with Cameron for almost an hour, sipping wine and watching the fiery colors deepen, then fade in the western sky. Neither spoke, content with the silence and the glowing spectacle before them, but his nearness unnerved her, forcing her to face her growing attraction to him.

In contrast to his surliness at their first encounter, his behavior that evening couldn't have been more relaxed, and again she wondered what had caused his change of attitude. She watched for signs of pity, thinking he might only feel sorry for her, stranded on his island without friends or family. And she remembered Mrs. Givens's threats to alert the authorities to his whereabouts if he wasn't kinder to his guest, but Celia knew of no reason why Cameron should fear the police.

The possible cause for his change in treatment of her that she found most appealing was that he had been drawn to her by the same magnetism that pulled her toward him. She hoped the events of the evening would present some clue to why he had finally decided to seek out her company.

When the first stars spangled the canopy of sky, Cameron took her hand and led her to the dining room. Twin candelabra filled with lighted tapers illuminated the room with soft light and revealed the snowy damask cloth and a silver epergne filled with sprays of sea oats, bougainvillea and delicate ferns. Translucent ivory china rimmed with gold, ornate silver flatware and stemmed crystal goblets marked places for two at one end of the long table. The setting could have been the dining room of an English manor house, except for the tropical, salt-scented breeze that stirred the draperies pulled back from the open French doors.

Cameron held her chair as she sat, then took his own at the head of the table. Mrs. Givens, wearing a sparkling white apron edged with lace for the occasion, carried a silver tureen in from the kitchen to the sideboard and ladled its contents into soup plates.

The housekeeper waited, hands folded across her immaculate apron, while Celia tasted the clear liquid.

"This is heavenly," Celia said. "You're a wonder, Mrs. Givens."

"Coquina broth. It's one of my specialties."

As if she'd been waiting for Celia's approval, the housekeeper hurried back to the kitchen.

Cameron set down his spoon and considered Celia with a smile. "Since you will be my guest for some weeks to come, I thought you would feel more comfortable here if we were better acquainted. Tell me about yourself. You told me your parents are no longer living?'' His amber eyes clouded, and his hand closed over hers. ''I know how painful it is to lose those close to you.'' He squeezed her fingers gently. ''What about other relatives? Friends? Is no one expecting your return?''

The warmth of his touch distracted her, making her ignore for the moment the motivation behind his questions. ''I have friends who've probably given me up for lost. Not to mention the customers in my bookstore.''

She caught herself before she said more. If she gave the impression no one was searching for her, would he refuse to let her leave, even when Captain Biggins arrived?

''And your fiancé?'' Cameron asked with obvious casualness.

''Fiancé?'' She had no desire to discuss Darren. The sooner she could erase that memory, the better.

''Or are you married?''

She shook her head. ''Had cold feet at the altar. Realized I was marrying for all the wrong reasons, so I ran. That's when my sailboat wrecked.''

''Regrets?'' His eyes studied her with a concentration that made her edgy.

''Only that I let matters go as far as they did. I was still in shock from my parents' deaths and not thinking straight.''

To her relief, Mrs. Givens chose that moment to bring in the main course, a magnificent baked grouper with new potatoes, carrots and green beans fresh from

Noah's garden. The housekeeper placed the tray in front of Cameron, and while he served, returned to the kitchen for hot rolls and fresh butter. The woman's competence amazed Celia. In a primitive kitchen with the barest of supplies, she served as fine a meal as any five-star restaurant.

"You live well on your island here in the middle of nowhere," Celia said to her host.

"Bis vivit qui bene vivit," he replied.

"He lives twice who lives well. Milton said the same. 'Nor love thy life, nor hate; but that thou liv'st, live well; how long or short permit to heaven.'"

"So you really do read Milton." A wry grin tugged at the corners of his attractive mouth.

Celia took a moment to realize he was referring to finding her with the upside-down copy of *Paradise Lost* in his office the previous week and couldn't stop the flush she felt spreading across her face.

"A wise man, Milton," Cameron said, ignoring her discomfort. "The quality of life must be more important than the length—although sometimes I wonder."

His eyes dimmed with pain, and his hand shook slightly as he sipped from his crystal goblet. She wondered if he was thinking of the brevity of the lives of his wife and son.

In the candlelight, his expression suddenly transformed, and he smiled, as if a mask had fallen over the unhappy man she'd glimpsed a moment before. With sudden clarity, she realized his moodiness had nothing to do with madness, as she'd first suspected when she'd ascribed Cameron's rapid change of moods to mental instability. Whenever his true feelings surfaced, Cameron erected a wall around himself she couldn't breach, always holding a part of himself secret, a man within the man, unknown and frightening, repelling her as surely as his outer self drew her to him.

"You surprise me with your knowledge of both Latin and Milton," he said congenially. "I didn't know Americans were trained in the classics."

"I've spent the majority of my life surrounded by books," she said. She felt an overwhelming desire to batter down the defenses he'd erected, to learn all she could about him. "Noah tells me you're a naturalist."

He nodded. "It passes the time. I study the swamps and coastal waters and record my observations. You'd be amazed at the flora and fauna in Florida."

"I live here, remember?"

"But have you ever stood among cypress trees a hundred and fifty feet high? Or walked among the other native hardwoods—red maple, swamp bay, pop ash and pond apple?"

"They must be very different from the trees of England."

His face, relaxed and alight with enthusiasm, was even more handsome than before. "I'm astonished every day when I consider the myriad plants here—ferns, marsh pinks, buttonbush and cocoplum, to name only a few, and dozens of species of bromeliads and orchids."

Celia's gaze fell on the spray of butterfly orchids

beside her plate, and his gift's significance grew with his words.

"And there're dozens of aquatic plants, too," he continued. "Bladderworts and waterlilies."

She grimaced. "Bladderwort. What a disgusting name."

He actually smiled then, an expression of such handsome sweetness, it took her breath away and intensified her longing to know more about Cameron's life before he came to America. "Did you have this interest in botany in England?"

His smile vanished. "No."

Cameron's abrupt change of mood unsettled her, and she turned the conversation back to his present studies in an effort to see him smile again. "What about wildlife, besides the obvious alligators and seabirds? Do you study it, too?"

He leaned forward, his enthusiasm returned. "The Everglades support an abundance of magnificent birds—wood storks, pileated woodpeckers, a variety of owls. And I've observed panthers and red wolves, black bear, white-tailed deer, bobcats, squirrels and raccoons—the list is endless."

"Do you hunt them?"

He looked embarrassed, as if she'd caught him in a weakness. "I can't bring myself to kill any of them. They're so beautiful, it seems wrong to harm them. We eat well from the gulf and have no need to hunt."

"I'd like to see it all for myself." She found his passion contagious. "Maybe you could take me with you some day."

The Everglades had their appeal, but the man who would be her guide made a potential excursion even more attractive.

At her request, a strange look flitted across his face, but was gone before she could assess whether it was puzzlement or revulsion. His enthusiasm for the plants and wildlife seemed genuine, but she guessed he used his knowledge to keep her at a safe distance and avoid any topic he found too personal.

Smiling his charming smile once more, he diverted her with small talk while they finished Mrs. Givens's meal, but underneath his beguiling exterior, she sensed a reserve, as if he were somehow afraid of her. When she tried to guess why he should fear her, she came up clueless.

Mrs. Givens saved her pièce de résistance for dessert. Bearing it before her like a treasure, she brought in a magnificent trifle with layers of delicate sponge cake, sliced bananas, pineapple chunks and grated coconut visible through the clear crystal bowl, all topped with mounds of thick whipped cream.

"My compliments, Mrs. Givens." Cameron finished the last bite of his trifle and laid his napkin aside. "You've outdone yourself this evening."

The housekeeper beamed at his praise. "It's a pleasure to cook for those who appreciate it."

Mrs. Givens kept her eyes lowered as she removed the plates, but Celia had the uncomfortable feeling the woman was observing them very carefully. What the housekeeper expected to see, Celia had no guess.

Cameron and Celia left Mrs. Givens clearing the

table and moved into the front room, where Cameron poured himself a brandy. Celia declined, remembering its effect on her the first night she met him. She had, however, a method to her abstinence. She hoped the alcohol would loosen his tongue and crumble the barriers he hid behind. During dessert, he'd talked of the weather and British politics, but had said nothing more about himself.

The portrait above the fern-filled fireplace caught her eye, and her question popped out before she could consider its consequences. "Do you miss them?"

"I miss Randolph very much."

His face couldn't have expressed more pain if she'd driven a stake through his heart. She noted, however, that he hadn't mentioned Clarissa. Afraid of treading further on dangerous ground and unsure what to say to crack his reserve without fueling his pain or anger, she remained silent.

"Do you dance, Celia?"

His rapid change of subject wasn't lost on her, an unsubtle signal that she had encroached onto a subject he preferred to avoid.

"Yes, a bit. I belonged to a cotillion when I was younger."

And she'd hated every minute of it. Awkward teenaged boys with sweaty palms had been forced to dance, even with a wallflower like her. Her mother had claimed the exercise would teach Celia social graces, but she'd hidden in the rest room of the hotel ballroom more often than she had participated and had learned only a great aversion to dancing.

Cameron set down his untouched brandy, picked up a massive carved wooden box from the sideboard, and tucked it under his arm. "Come."

He took her hand and pulled her after him. The warmth of his bare flesh pressed against hers sent shivers of pleasure through her, and she wondered if he experienced the same effect. On the darkened veranda, he placed the box on a table, wound a large key protruding from its side, and opened the lid.

The tinkling music of an unfamiliar waltz floated onto the night air, blending with the gentle pounding of the distant surf and the soughing of wind through the trees. It was a night made for lovers, and she realized with a start that she might be falling in love with Cameron Alexander.

He held his arms open. "Dance with me, Celia."

Without hesitation, she raised her hand to his, placed the other on his broad shoulder, and was drawn into his embrace. With a natural grace, he waltzed her up and down the broad porch, through the rectangles of lamplight cast through the tall windows onto the weathered wood of the floor.

The imprint of his hand burned like a brand at her waist while the silvery, tumbling notes of the antique music box scattered like stardust on the night air. He didn't hold her in a clenched embrace, but at arm's length, so that she could watch his face while they twirled slowly up the veranda and back again.

"Cameron—"

"Don't speak," he said gently. "Don't spoil it."

Her heart yearned to know him better, to learn what

made the enigma before her tick, what dreams he dreamed, what devils he wrestled, but she held her questions for another time and watched a gamut of emotions cross his face. She counted pain, desire and even amusement among them.

They paused only long enough to rewind the music box, then fell again into a loose embrace and began their leisurely waltz once more.

The music wound down, and the case clock chimed the hour in the front room. Although the dance had ended, Cameron held her in his arms and pulled her close. She tilted her head and lifted her lips, willing recipients, toward his. Her breath caught in her throat as he leaned toward her, but abruptly he drew back, clasped both her hands in his and crushed them to his lips.

"Good night." His words came out in a strangled tone, and he turned and left her standing alone in the moonlight.

When her reeling senses had steadied, Celia stepped quietly into the hallway and paused at the door to the front room. A dejected Cameron sat on the sofa, gazing at the portrait above the mantel, his fingers curled around an empty brandy snifter.

Celia climbed the stairs to her room, slipped out of her dress and toppled into bed. She expected to toss and turn, but fell instantly asleep. She dreamed of a man with a tortured expression who danced her across a floor painted with the portrait of his dead wife.

Chapter Seven

Celia awoke the next morning with conflicting emotions. Part of her yearned for the weeks to pass quickly so she could return home to her friends and business. But another part of her desired nothing more than to spend the rest of her days with Cameron on his island. She had detected a flicker of response from him the night before and believed that time might fan that flicker into a flame. She sang as she dressed for breakfast, something she hadn't done since her arrival.

She found Mrs. Givens in the kitchen, scowling into her teacup.

"You didn't tire yourself out last night?" Celia asked. The woman had to be at least in her sixties, and preparing such a meal without the usual conveniences had been a grueling task.

"What?" The housekeeper looked up as if her mind were wrapped in fog.

"Are you all right?"

Mrs. Givens rose from the table and refilled her cup before sitting once more. Her age-spotted hands trembled. "It's nothing, m'dear. Just my sixth sense running amok today."

She attempted a smile, but her expression wavered, and Celia feared the kind old woman would burst into tears.

"What sixth sense?" Celia asked.

"It's a curse, it is, passed down to me from my old grandmother on my mother's side. She could see the future. Look straight into a person's eyes and read their fate."

"You can do that?" Celia struggled to keep the skepticism from her voice. Mrs. Givens seemed upset enough without having her beliefs questioned.

"Would be better if I could. Grandma could see a person's destiny as clear as looking through a window. She knew the day that World War II would end and predicted the day to the hour that the old king would die."

"That's some talent. Did you forecast my arrival here?"

"Wish I was good enough for that. With me, I see only shapes and colors, and I don't always know who they're meant for."

Celia humored the old woman's fantasies but didn't buy the clairvoyance she spoke of. "And do you see something now?"

Mrs. Givens's stout shoulders shuddered. "Last time I had a premonition like this was when Clarissa and Randolph went off to Devon—"

She clapped a plump hand over her mouth, and her

eyes registered her horror at speaking aloud the very names she had warned Celia not to utter.

Celia tried to make light of the woman's worries. "Maybe there's a physical explanation for the way you feel, like a dropping barometer at an approaching storm."

The housekeeper shook her head. "The feelings are too strong, the colors too dark—"

She spoke in a keening moan, and Celia felt the hairs rise on the back of her neck. Mrs. Givens must have seen the uneasiness on her face, because she leaned over and patted her hand. When she spoke again, her voice had resumed its no-nonsense tone.

"I hope you're right, m'dear—although I don't relish a storm here. If the wind don't blow us away, the waves could wash us out to sea. It'd be the end of me, because I never learned to swim."

"Let me teach you." Although talk of storms resurrected the horrible memories Celia had managed to tamp down into her subconscious, she was glad to abandon talk of premonitions and omens. And she was serious about the swimming lessons. They would help pass the time.

"Swim?" Mrs. Givens shook her head. "An old woman like me?"

"It would be good for you. The gulf water is still warm and pleasant this time of year, and the salt will buoy you."

Mrs. Givens sniffed. "I haven't time for such foolishness."

Celia finished her breakfast in silence, and she forgot completely Mrs. Givens's forecast of doom when Cameron entered the kitchen.

"Do you still wish to see everything for yourself?" he asked Celia.

"Everything?" Celia stammered, thinking he referred to her earlier rummaging through his desk.

"I thought you might like to sail through the mangrove islands today."

She remembered their conversation at dinner the night before when she had expressed her desire to see the islands and the Everglades. She remembered, too, his dejected posture later, slouched before the portrait, mourning his wife and child. Maybe this morning's invitation was a sign that he was beginning to put the past behind him.

Mrs. Givens turned from her dishwashing and studied them both with bright eyes. Celia felt a spasm of guilt at leaving the housekeeper to do all the work while Celia played sightseer.

"There's sewing to finish," Celia said, "and I should help Mrs. Givens with her chores—"

"Don't you fret about me, m'dear. I'll just put together a lunch for the two of you."

"Splendid, Mrs. Givens," Cameron said.

Had Darren uttered the word *splendid,* Celia would have laughed at his swishiness, but in a deep tone that discouraged ridicule and sent a thrill through her bones, Cameron managed to make the word sound both masculine and enthusiastic.

Less than an hour later, with the handle of a full picnic basket tucked over her arm and Mrs. Givens's wide-brimmed straw hat shading her face from the sun, Celia walked with Cameron down the garden path toward the pier.

Noah worked on the sandy path to his cottage, sweeping the sand into neat patterns with a bamboo rake.

"I'll be taking the skiff today, Mr. Alex," he called. "Got to gather grass for the cow, but I'll be back before dark."

"Take care, Noah. You never know when you might run into a marine patrol," Cameron warned.

"Don't you worry about old Noah," the handyman said with a hearty laugh. "Ain't no going back for me now. I'll keep a good eye out."

Cameron climbed into the sailboat, took the basket and placed it under a seat. Celia placed her hands on his broad shoulders, and he grasped her waist and lifted her down into the boat. Her skin burned beneath her clothes where he'd touched her, and she regretted when he let her go.

She settled onto a seat, and the boat slipped out of sight of Solitaire and Mrs. Givens. Luxuriating in the open air, Celia lifted her face toward the full blast of the sun.

Cameron smiled at her and shook his head.

"Why are you smiling?"

"Because you are such an unusual woman."

"Why do you say that?"

"Most other women I've known—" His smile faded and his voice faltered.

"Yes?"

"They're always fretting about their complexions, their clothes and their hair."

She felt a prick of discomfort, wondering if her casual Florida ways made her seem coarse and unmannerly. She patted her hair self-consciously and tucked her battered sneakers underneath her borrowed skirt in an effort to appear more ladylike.

"Don't," he said.

"Don't what?" She wasn't accustomed to feeling awkward and unsure of herself.

"Don't change anything. Be yourself, because you are the most refreshing woman I've ever met."

She wasn't sure if that was a compliment. In the past six years, she was the *only* woman he had met.

But she couldn't stay worried on such a day, with a brilliant blue, cloud-free sky, low humidity and enough breeze to fill the sails. She had not set foot off Solitaire since her escape attempt, and the newfound freedom exhilarated her.

She could tell by looking at Cameron that he felt the same. He became a different person on the water as she watched his stiffness and reserve disappear with the breeze that ruffled his thick, golden hair and the sunshine that burnished the dynamic planes of his face. She couldn't reconcile the dejected man she'd witnessed the previous night in front of his family's portrait with the free spirit before her now. She liked this Cameron much better, even more than the one who had kissed her hands on the veranda not so many hours ago.

He turned the sailboat east and threaded his way

among the hundreds of tiny islands that dotted the coast. She'd never been especially brilliant at geography, but her best guess placed Solitaire somewhere south of Cape Romano in the Ten Thousand Islands Aquatic Preserve, one of the last great wildernesses left in the state.

They sailed for almost two hours through an endless maze of bays, channels and islands.

"How can you tell where we are?" she asked.

"I know these waters like the back of my hand. Every island is different. I'll show you."

He lowered the sail and pulled alongside a protrusion in the water, little more than a sandbar and shoals where a few young mangroves balanced delicately on spiderlike branches on the limestone of oyster shells.

"This is how an island begins," he explained. "Alongshore currents from the north carry quartz sand and deposit it in deeper water parallel to the shore. As the sand deposits build nearer the surface, the oysters colonize."

Celia peered into the clear water beside the boat.

"You can see it there." He moved next to her, placed his arm around her shoulders to steady her, and pointed.

As she studied the area where the limestone mixed with other sediments, pushing out of the water at low tide high enough that the mangroves could take hold, she had difficulty concentrating. Her pulse hummed at the warmth of his flesh against hers, and the intoxicating male scent of him stirred her senses. He released her too soon for her liking and reached over the side, scooping a long, green cigar-shaped pod from the water.

"This is a red mangrove seed," he said. "Carried by the tide, it eventually takes root in the sediments on an oyster bar, like that one."

She looked to the spindly tree with its arched prop roots that stretched into the sand like the extended legs of a gigantic spider.

"Because of their strange roots," he explained, "and the way they appear to walk out across the shallow tidal zones, the Seminoles named the red mangroves 'walking trees.'"

His enthusiasm reminded her of Kevin Jordan, the tiny eight-year-old with a passion for dinosaurs whose mother had brought him every Saturday morning to Sand Castles to buy the latest book on the creatures. Kevin's infatuation was like a religion to him, and he converted everyone he met with his zeal for the prehistoric beasts. Convinced by the little boy's careful explanations and transfixed by the ardor in his eyes, Celia had come to love the beasts herself.

Cameron's obvious love of his surroundings had the same effect on her. She couldn't imagine anyone spending a day with him in the Ten Thousand Islands and coming away untouched by his knowledge and enthusiasm. He was an extraordinary teacher, and his love of the land and water was contagious. He had exposed another facet of himself there among the mangrove islands, a side that intrigued and fascinated her.

He pushed the boat off the oyster bar, raised the

sail, and headed toward one of the denser islands to the south. As they approached it, Celia spotted a sandy beach where the water lapped instead of breaking, shaded by tall trees whose slender trunks were capped with a profusion of small, deep green leaves. Cameron turned the boat straight in, lowered the sail once more, and beached the boat on the sand beneath the canopy of shade.

She tilted her head back and gazed into the overlapping branches high above her. "They're beautiful. Almost regal."

"These are mangroves, too."

"But their trunks are straight and tall. No monkeybar roots. How can these be mangroves without the arching root system?"

"These are black mangroves. They grow better in areas more protected from the wind and waves. Come ashore, and we'll have a better look."

"And you called *me* unusual," Celia said with a laugh. "I've never seen anyone as passionate about mangroves as you are."

His eyes burned into hers and his tone turned intimate and teasing. "And what *should* I feel passionately about?"

Me, she longed to say, but couldn't. She was the first to look away, unsure of what she saw in the depth of his gaze.

Cameron pulled off his boots and rolled his pants legs above his knees. She looked down at her sneakers, the single pair of shoes she owned. She didn't want to ruin them in the saltwater, but she also feared slicing her feet on shells if she took them off.

As if reading her mind, Cameron said, "Don't bother to take off your shoes."

Without warning, she felt herself swept up in his powerful arms. She clasped her arms around his neck and saw the smile tugging at the corner of his mouth.

The warmth of his body generated a heat within her own, and she longed to press her lips against the upturned corners of his mouth. At that moment, she feared that she had fallen irrevocably in love with the mysterious Cameron Alexander.

He carried her onto the beach well above the high tide mark and set her on her feet. Reluctantly, she dropped her arms from around his neck. If holding her against his heart had stirred him in any way, he didn't show it. Maybe his love for the long-dead Clarissa shielded him from other attractions. Except for the brush of his lips against her forehead the night he had rescued her, and the kiss on the back of her hands the night before, Cameron had been only a host, at some times more gracious than others, but nothing more.

"Let me show you the rest of the island," he said in a calm voice that contrasted sharply with the wild racing of her heart.

They threaded their way through the broad sandy spaces beneath the mangroves to slightly higher ground, where Cameron pointed out white mangroves. The names red, black and white confused her, because all had grayish-brown trunks and deep green leaves. Mixed in with the white mangroves were the buttonwood trees.

"The buttonwood is not a true mangrove," he continued in his relaxed, scholarly tone, "but it is salt-tolerant and commonly found in most mangrove forests."

They plunged toward the island's interior through thickets of trees. She recognized wax myrtles and towering sea grape and cabbage palms. The others Cameron identified as gumbo limbo, strangler fig, red bay and gray nickerbean. At times he took her arm to lead her safely away from the thorny perils of cat-claw and Hercules'-club or to prevent her slipping over treacherous strands of a wiry cactus, but she could read nothing but politeness in his gesture.

"How did you learn about all this?" she asked.

"From the books Captain Biggins brings me."

"You should write a book of your own." She thought of the tourists who had thronged her shop, always hungry for more information about the Sunshine State.

"I keep records," he said. "Perhaps one day when I am too old to sail anything but a desk, I'll put all this knowledge into book form."

"Why wait?"

"To be honest," Cameron said, "I fear if others learn of the beauty here, too many will come to visit and it will all be ruined." He scowled at the unpleasant prospect. "We can't linger here. There are other islands I want to show you."

He led the way back to the boat, stopping now and

then to point out mangrove periwinkles—tree snails with brilliantly colored shells—fiddler crabs and even a raccoon making an early lunch of a horseshoe crab.

When they reached the beach, again he scooped her into his arms and carried her through the shallow water to the boat. When he reached the bow, he didn't release her, but stood with her in his arms and gazed into her eyes.

"Celia—"

She held her breath, hoping he would give some clue to his feelings for her.

"When I noticed your reluctance to ruin your shoes, your only pair," he said, "I thought of all the things you have done without since your arrival here, of the friends who must be missing you, of your bookstore that needs your attention."

Captivated by the look in his amber eyes, she couldn't speak.

"I've been terribly selfish," he said, "thinking only of myself and my desire for seclusion, but I intend to rectify that situation now."

She waited, still saying nothing, hoping for words of affection, of some sign that he was beginning to care for her as she did for him.

"To prove to you that I'm not the selfish ogre you must think and that I can place your welfare above my own—"

She peered into his eyes, trying to read his feelings, wanting to cup her hand against the strength of his square jaw.

"—tomorrow," he said, "we'll leave before dawn, and I'll sail you to Key West as you wish."

CAMERON SET CELIA IN the boat, pushed it from its anchorage near the sandy beach, and hopped aboard. She sat in the bow, facing him, unable to speak, her mind whirling as she struggled with her conflicting emotions. Part of her longed for home, but a stronger part wanted to remain on the island with Cameron.

Unaware of her turmoil, Cameron raised the sail and set a westward course through the islands toward the gulf.

She wondered at his change of heart. Had he really repented of what he called his selfishness, or did he simply want the solitude of his island back as it had been before her arrival? Her spirits plummeted with her hopes. While she had come to admire the man and the life he lived, she wondered if he'd found her presence so intrusive, he would risk exposing his secret hideaway in order to be rid of her.

The beauty of the islands helped distract her from her troublesome thoughts. Silver mullet flashed in the sunlight as they leaped into the air, and soon playful dolphins chased behind the boat in hot pursuit of a mullet meal.

Celia looked up to find Cameron studying her and decided to tell him the truth. "I don't want to leave here."

His face broke into a wide, delighted smile, looking as if she'd paid him a personal compliment. "I know what you mean. Sometimes I spend days and nights

among the islands, returning to Solitaire only to prevent Mrs. Givens from worrying herself ill and sending Noah to find me.''

"I meant that I don't want to leave Solitaire."

The look he gave her seemed to probe her very
soul. She finally turned away from the intensity in his
eyes, but he said nothing.

As they neared the gulf, Cameron dropped anchor
off a narrow key rimmed with sparkling white quartz
sand with a line of natural dunes above the stretch of
beach. He gathered the picnic basket, a roll of canvas
and a blanket and carried them into the dunes, where
he deposited them beneath a trio of cabbage palms.
Then he returned for her.

She placed her arms around his neck as he lifted
her from the boat. Her hands slid across the firm muscles of his back, and she felt the pressure of his arms
beneath her legs. When he reached the beach and set
her on her feet, she didn't let go, but pulled his un-
resisting head toward hers and kissed him, molding
her body to his with an abandon she had never felt
before.

He flinched as if in surprise for the briefest second
before his mouth closed fiercely on hers. She tasted
the salt on his lips and relished the hard length of his
body against her own. Her head filled with a furious
roar, and she couldn't tell if it was the blood pounding
there or the surf crashing on the beach.

If he carried through with his intentions to take her
to Key West, she thought, she would at least have
today to remember.

With a jerk, he pulled away and held her at arm's length. "God in heaven, Celia, don't do this."

She looked up into eyes like pools of misery. "I think I'm falling in love with you, Cameron."

He released her and stood staring with an expression she couldn't fathom. He lifted his hand and with his index finger slowly traced the curve of her cheek and the fullness of her lips, still throbbing from contact with his own. His touch sent a shudder of pleasure through her, but before she could respond, he turned away and walked into the dunes.

His actions were so contradictory, she didn't know what to think. Her heart believed that he felt as she did, but if that were true, her head argued, why did he turn from her and why did he insist that she leave the next day?

She followed him into the dunes and watched as he fastened the canvas like an awning between the palms. In the shade it created, he spread the blanket and set the picnic basket on it.

"Are you hungry?" His matter-of-fact tone spoke louder than his words, warning her not to indulge her emotions.

Still confused by his behavior, Celia knelt before the basket and began unpacking the lunch Mrs. Givens had prepared. At the sight and smell of it, she realized the morning's activities had given her an appetite undented by the turmoil in her heart.

Cameron sat crosslegged beside her, and she handed him a sandwich wrapped in a linen napkin and took one for herself. The thick wedges of homemade bread had been spread with butter and mustard and filled with slices of sharp cheddar and leaves of crisp lettuce.

As Celia ate, she considered her plight. She didn't want to leave Solitaire. The main reason munched contentedly beside her. She needed to learn more about Cameron to better her chance of convincing him to allow her to stay.

She planned her questions, hoping to lead him slowly into more personal topics. "Have you always loved the out-of-doors?"

He leaned back on his elbows and stared out across the brilliant green waters of the gulf. The sea breeze lifted his sun-streaked hair from the broad expanse of his tanned forehead and exposed a jagged white scar at the hairline.

"When I was a boy, summer holidays were my favorite time of year. We left London where Father had his offices and went to Devon where he owned farms and a manor house. I played the entire time along the shore, climbing rock cliffs and exploring caves."

Celia remembered from the newspaper clipping that Clarissa and Randolph had been murdered in Devon and thought how tragic that his place of happiest memories also held his saddest.

His eyes took on the faraway glaze of memory, and she wished she could see pictures of him as a boy. Maybe he had looked like young Randolph in the portrait above the mantel, handsome and appealing with his mischievous smile.

"I pretended I was a ferocious pirate," he said with a smile, "burying treasure in the recesses of the cliff caves. Exploring the caves was forbidden, of course."

"Dangerous?"

"In many ways. I could have become lost or trapped by an incoming tide."

"Weren't you frightened?"

He threw back his head and laughed with a warm, hearty sound that drove a night heron from his perch in the palm above them and sent it squawking down the beach. "The prohibition and the danger made it all the more exciting. With the invulnerability of youth, I never really believed that anything bad could happen to me."

"You must have been a trial for Mrs. Givens."

His laughter faded and his face clouded. "I have caused that poor woman more than her share of pain, yet she has always loved me as a mother would, nonetheless."

"Do you miss your work in England?" Celia tried to ask casually, knowing she treaded closer to dangerous ground.

He finished the last of his sandwich, wiped his mouth with the linen napkin, and then rummaged through the basket, coming up with a ladyfinger banana. "I hated working in the mining offices, trapped behind a desk every day, dealing with a thousand problems and people who seemed to create difficulties when they should have been resolving them."

She watched, mesmerized by the beauty of his

strong hands as he peeled back the yellow skin of the banana, bit off a piece and chewed it fiercely.

"And the farms in Devon?" she asked.

He finished the fruit, dug a hole in the sand, and buried the peel. "I would have spent all my time there if I could, but they were ably managed, farmed by men whose families had been there for generations. The mines took almost all my attention from the time I finished university."

"That was a young age to be put in charge."

"What choice did I have? My father was dead, and the business was mine. I began work the day I left Oxford and never quit until—" He fell silent.

Gathering her courage, Celia plunged into the question she'd wanted most to ask from the beginning. "Do you miss her?"

"Who?" He would not look at her, but lay back and covered his face with his forearm.

Celia wanted to see his eyes when she said the name, but they were hidden from her. "Clarissa."

"I do not speak of her. Ever."

Her feet were planted solidly on dangerous ground then, but with the prospect of leaving Solitaire the next day, Celia felt she had nothing to lose by forging ahead. "Sometimes it helps ease the pain to talk of those we've lost."

"I cannot." He spit the angry words at her, but he did not move, and she saw a tear slip from the corner of his eye and roll across his cheek.

Stymied in her attempt to learn more of his relationship with Clarissa and remorseful that she had caused him pain, she gave up the conversation and busied herself repacking the picnic basket.

Her heart ached at the thought of his love for Clarissa and the pain her death must have caused him. Celia would have given anything to have him love *her* with such faithfulness.

When she'd finished putting away the remnants of lunch, Cameron still stretched out upon the blanket with his arm thrown across his face. She could tell from his steady breathing and the rise and fall of his chest that he'd fallen asleep. She sat for a while, drinking in the sight of him, storing it in her memory against the day when she would never see him again.

The trilling call of a pileated woodpecker in the tree above her broke her reverie and turned her attention back to her surroundings. She gazed toward the gulf where a tall stand of Spanish bayonet with creamy blossoms framed the delicate sea oats and prickly pear cactus between her and the wide, white beach, fully exposed at low tide. Seaside purslane, inkberry and railroad vine held the sand fast against the dune and added splashes of green, yellow and pink to the canvas before her. She felt like a stranger in paradise.

The warm sun made her drowsy, and she looked back to the sleeping Cameron. The end of her time with him was fast approaching, and she longed to make the best of it. She pulled off her shoes and lay beside him. He stirred at her movements and turned on his side toward her. As easily as coming home, she curved her body into his, pulled his arm around her waist, and fell asleep.

Sometime later, the slanting rays of the sun slipped beneath the sheltering canvas and beat upon her face. She awakened with a start, alone. She could see the sailboat anchored beyond the surf, but Cameron was nowhere in sight.

She tugged on her sneakers and set off down the beach, following his footprints in the sand. Several hundred yards away, she found him, sitting on a dune with his elbows on his knees and gazing out to sea. He stood when he saw her, brushed sand from his clothes, and walked to meet her.

Celia ran to him, and he lifted her in his arms, kissing her as fiercely as he had before. She twined her hands in his hair, holding him fast, yielding to the pressure of his lips on hers, rejoicing in the strength of his embrace.

Too soon the kiss ended, and, breathless, she gazed up at him. "Tell me now that you don't love me." Triumph filled her voice.

His eyes burned into hers. "With God as my witness, I love you, Celia."

He crushed her to him once more, and when he spoke, she could feel his lips against her hair and his breath on her cheek. "But love isn't enough. It can't save you."

The solemnness in his tone frightened her, and she pulled back and scanned his face. "What do you mean?"

"You must run from this place as fast as you can,

Celia Stevens. Flee for your life—while I still possess the strength to let you go.''

"I don't understand."

"Because I do love you, tomorrow I will take you to Key West and leave you there. You must forget you ever met me."

"No!" She dug her fingers into his arm and shook him. "I will never forget you. Why must you send me away?"

She began to cry in hoarse, choking sobs, trying to comprehend his actions, his reasoning, and failing utterly.

"You must go for your own safety," he said.

"Safety from what?"

Cameron said nothing and wouldn't look her in the eyes.

"I'm safer here," she insisted, "than anywhere else in the world."

He pulled away and stalked down the beach into the breaking surf. Mindless of the saltwater soaking her shoes and the hem of her skirt, Celia followed.

"I'm begging you, Cameron, please let me stay. I'll share your exile with you."

He stood in the surf, gazing westward, for what seemed an eternity. Then he leaned over and splashed his face with seawater. When he finally spoke, his voice was mechanical, stripped of all emotion. "We must start back if we're to reach Solitaire by dark. And you must get to bed immediately tonight. We'll leave before dawn in the morning."

He strode back up the beach, gathered the canvas,

blanket and basket, and loaded them into the boat. With her shoes and skirt already waterlogged, Celia didn't wait for his assistance. She climbed aboard on her own and huddled into the bow for her long, final ride, back to Solitaire.

Chapter Eight

Cameron hadn't counted on falling in love with Celia Stevens, although he should have recognized the danger the day he rescued her from the beach. From that moment on, her beauty and courage had tugged at his heart, regenerating feelings he'd thought forever dead. He'd spent more time with her because he'd wanted to, couldn't keep away from her any longer, no matter how hard he tried.

Loving her as he did, he admitted reluctantly, he had only one acceptable course of action.

Avoiding Celia's gaze in an effort to maintain his determination to send her away, Cameron steered the sailboat toward home. His emotions fought to overcome the rationale of his resolve. Sending her away would be the hardest thing he'd ever had to do. She had brought him back to life after so many years of numbness and despair. His days would be empty again without her vivaciousness, her self-reliance, her spirit, and most of all, the radiance of her smile and the music of her voice.

After only a few miles, she moved and sat beside

him, close enough that she didn't have to shout above the wind.

"Why can't I be safe on Solitaire?" she insisted.

He struggled to think of a plausible reason. He couldn't tell her the truth. "It's too isolated. If you were to become hurt or ill—"

"You and Mrs. Givens take that risk."

"It's our choice."

"And if *I* choose to stay?"

"I can't accept that responsibility."

Her eyes, as changeable and beautiful as the gulf waters, scoured his face. "Can't or won't?"

Fighting the desire to pull her into his arms and keep her with him always, he looked away. "Both."

"But if you love me—"

"Because I love you, I will do everything in my power to protect you."

"I'm a grown woman. I don't need protecting. I can take care of myself."

For a moment he almost believed that she could. Then he remembered Clarissa and Randolph, and his determination hardened. "I've made up my mind. There's no changing it now, Celia. You might as well save your breath."

His frustration gave his voice a hard edge, and she flinched at his words. He wanted to soften them, but thought better of it. She would leave more willingly if she believed him angry with her.

And she had to leave. Her life depended on it.

The fight seemed to leave her, and she withdrew into herself. They sailed for hours through the labyrinth of channels and bays that surrounded the emerald mangrove islands, but they might as well have been moving through darkness for all the attention either of them paid to the world around them. Neither spoke, and the uneasy silence lay between them like a stone wall.

The wind dropped late in the afternoon, and Cameron had to make long, sweeping tacks to take them back to Solitaire. As a result, night fell while they were still miles away, and the stars had been out for hours when Cameron finally secured the sailboat to his dock.

Refusing his help, Celia climbed out onto the pier. The boards rumbled with the pounding of feet, and Mrs. Givens approached, like a schooner under full sail.

"Praise God! You're back." She stopped beside Celia and fanned her plump face with her apron as she caught her breath.

"Of course we are." The words were the first Cameron had spoken in hours. "You mustn't allow our delay to upset you so. The wind failed us, or we'd have been here sooner."

"Isn't you I'm worried about," the housekeeper said. "It's Noah. He should have been back early this afternoon, and I've seen no sign of him."

Even in the darkness Cameron could read the concern that contorted the old woman's face.

"Maybe he's run away," Celia suggested. "Maybe the loneliness here finally got to him."

"Run away to be taken in by the law?" Mrs. Givens asked. "Not likely he'd chance that. I fear he's been picked up by the marine patrol—or worse still, lying sick or injured alone in the Everglades."

"Get me a lantern and some water," Cameron said. "Noah cuts grass on a dry prairie a mile or so inland. I'll look for him there."

Mrs. Givens scurried back to the kitchen, and Cameron, anxious for the well-being of his friend, raced to the front of the house and went inside.

CONVINCED THE TWO OF THEM had forgotten her, Celia sat at the edge of the dock, dangled her feet above the low tide, and worried about the gentle black man who had treated her so kindly. A hundred things could have happened to him—snakebite, sudden illness, a fatal machete cut, drowning or an attack by wild animals—and now Cameron was heading into the darkness to face the same perils.

His footfalls on the deck alerted her to his return, and she stood to face him. "I'm going with you."

He shook his head, his handsome jaw set in a firm line. "You'll only slow me down. If Noah is injured, the sooner I can reach him, the sooner I can help him."

She longed to accompany him, not only to aid in the search but to spend every minute possible with Cameron before he took her to Key West. But the stubborn set of his mouth convinced her his mind was made up about going alone, and she abandoned her insistence.

Cameron had donned a leather jacket, a broad-brimmed hat and boots that reached to his knees. A heavy pistol was thrust in his belt. He patted the weapon. "The mate to this is in the bottom drawer of my desk, loaded and ready to fire, and a loaded rifle is hanging on the wall of my bedroom. If any stranger sets foot on the island while I'm gone, don't hesitate to defend yourself."

He clambered into the boat. Mrs. Givens returned with bottles of water and a lantern. Without looking back, he pushed the boat away from the dock, raised the sail, and headed through the darkness toward the mainland.

"Now I have two to worry over," the housekeeper said with a sigh.

Full of worry herself, Celia placed her arm around the woman's shoulders, and together they returned to the house.

"How can you be certain Noah didn't just decide to leave for good?" Celia asked.

"Remember the feeling I had this morning that something terrible was about to happen? I don't think I would have felt that way if Noah was only going to desert us. He must be hurt."

Celia had no reason to trust Mrs. Givens's premonitions. "I don't suppose he left a note or anything?"

She shook her head. "I checked his house. All of his things are still there."

They entered the kitchen where Mrs. Givens made tea and tried to convince Celia to eat something, but the knot in her throat made swallowing impossible.

She ached for Noah in danger in the Everglades and for Cameron, but most of all, she mourned her own loss. Cameron's search might delay her departure for a day or two, but as soon as Cameron returned, with or without Noah, she would be leaving Solitaire for good.

"Get yourself up to bed, m'dear," Mrs. Givens said. "You're all wore out. I'll waken you if Mr. Alexander returns."

Celia was too tired to disagree. She climbed the stairs to her bedroom, undressed and pulled on her nightgown, but her mind raced with memories of all that had happened that day, and she knew she couldn't sleep. She pulled the rocking chair from her room onto the veranda, thinking to rock herself into slumber, but the open doors to Cameron's room caught her attention. She abandoned her chair and entered his room.

Shameless in her desire to learn all she could of the man who'd claimed he loved her, she lit the lamp on the dresser. The evidence of Mrs. Givens's handiwork was everywhere, from the freshly swept oriental carpet and polished furniture to the vase of fresh flowers on the dresser, but the room held little imprint of its occupant.

In a tray on the bureau lay silver-backed brushes with strands of golden hair caught among the bristles, a porcelain shaving mug and a long razor with a brass guard. The drawers held stacks of linen handkerchiefs, soft white shirts and undergarments, and socks in both cotton and silk. Nothing told her any more of Cameron Alexander than she already knew.

She opened the tall armoire and inspected the row of slacks and jackets that hung there. Pressing her face into the fabrics, she inhaled leather, saddle soap and pipe tobacco, combined with the distinctive scent of Cameron himself. Rows of polished boots lined the bottom of the closet, and on the top shelf stood a row of hats. She was closing the door when she caught sight of a box shoved behind the headgear. After pulling a chair over to the closet, she stood on its seat, moved the hats aside, and withdrew a leather container the size of a dress box.

Sitting on the bed, she opened the box. Inside she found a baby's christening gown, fashioned of long tiers of delicate batiste and lace, and a tiny lace cap. Beneath them nestled a silver cup engraved with the name *Randolph,* a small toy dog on wheels, carved from wood, and a little boy's sweater, knitted from navy blue yarn. At the bottom of the box lay a long, white envelope, unsealed. Inside, she discovered several locks of blond curls.

Her heart ached for Cameron as she surveyed his souvenirs, all he had left of his son. She repacked them carefully and returned the treasures to their hiding place. She looked for other boxes, but there were no other keepsakes, nothing at all in Cameron's room to give any indication that Clarissa Alexander had ever existed.

After blowing out the light, Celia returned to her chair on the veranda, wondering why Cameron had preserved so many memories of his son but none of his wife. He had refused even to speak of her. Did he fear that by loving Celia he was being unfaithful to Clarissa's memory, and had that fear motivated him to remove her from Solitaire with all haste?

Cameron was a puzzle Celia had been unable to solve, and she was unlikely to have more of a chance. Even if she managed to find out what made him tick, she thought with a deep sigh of frustration, it would do her little good. Within days she'd be out of his life forever.

"Celia?" Mrs. Givens spoke behind her, and Celia started with surprise.

The housekeeper placed a reassuring hand on her shoulder. "Didn't mean to frighten you, m'dear. I just came up to see that you're all right."

"I can't sleep, not until Cameron's back safe and sound."

"Come down to the kitchen with me," Mrs. Givens said. "I've a cheery fire going and a boiling kettle for a fresh pot of tea. We can pass the time together until Cameron returns—or we fall asleep in spite of ourselves."

An approaching thunderstorm, her worry over Cameron, and her sorrow over her imminent departure made Celia hungry for companionship. She wrapped a shawl over her gown and followed Mrs. Givens downstairs.

The kitchen provided a bright, comfortable haven for their vigil. They sat before the fire, sewing and sipping tea, while the storm rumbled in from the gulf.

When the wind increased, Mrs. Givens closed the French doors on the kitchen's west side. Soon, blowing rain spattered against the panes.

Suddenly Mrs. Givens cried out. Celia followed the woman's horrified gaze and saw Noah standing in the opening of the east French doors. The whiteness of his eyes glimmered wildly in the lamplight, and a dark bundle was slung across his shoulders. He moved quickly into the kitchen and dumped his burden onto the kitchen table.

As Noah turned back the corner of his canvas bundle, the flickering light of the fire revealed Cameron's unconscious form.

Her heart pounding with fear, Celia rushed to him. "Is he dead?"

She felt for a pulse at his neck and almost collapsed with relief when she felt the strength of its beat beneath her fingers.

"He's alive, but mighty sick," Noah said. "I had to range farther than usual to find grass. On my way back, I spotted Mr. Alex's boat floating in the channel with its sails luffing in the wind. Mr. Alex was lying in the bottom of the boat, too sick to move."

Celia placed her wrist against Cameron's forehead. "He's burning with fever. We can't leave him here. Carry him to his bed, please, Noah. Mrs. Givens, bring extra blankets."

The housekeeper stood in the far corner of the kitchen, her eyes wide with fright. She hadn't moved since Noah had carried in Cameron. "Is he going to die?"

"Not if I can help it," Celia vowed. "We should send Noah for a doctor."

"No!" Mrs. Givens response was immediate and forceful. "Mr. Alexander would rather die—"

"Don't be ridiculous," Celia said in disbelief. "He has a raging fever, and it could be anything from West Nile virus to pneumonia or malaria. Without a doctor and a medical lab, we won't know how to treat him."

"I have aspirin," Mrs. Givens insisted, "and my herbs, but no doctors. Isn't that right, Noah?"

Sadness etched the man's ebony features. "She's right, Miss Celia. Mr. Alex don't want nobody knowing where he's at."

Disgusted by their refusal to send for help, Celia shook her head. "Then I'll have to care for him as best I can. Just bring me what I need."

Noah lifted Cameron tenderly in his strong arms, and Celia followed them up the stairs. She jerked back the covers on Cameron's bed, and Noah laid him on the fresh sheets, then tugged off his boots while she removed his rain-sodden clothes. Cameron shivered with the fever, and she pulled the covers quickly over his naked body.

"Is he gonna be all right, Miss Celia?"

"If I can keep him cool and comfortable, he will be."

Her words were brave, but she had no idea how to treat his unknown illness. Silently she promised Cameron that she'd keep him alive if only by the strength of her will.

Mrs. Givens appeared at the door with an armload of blankets and a bucket of water. She set them on the dresser, then gathered up Cameron's discarded clothes.

Celia poured cool water into a basin and bathed Cameron's face.

His eyes fluttered open, and he gazed at her. "Clarissa? My head hurts."

In his delirium, he was calling for his dead wife, not Celia.

"No, it's me, Celia. You're going to be fine. Just try to sleep."

She felt his burning forehead and turned to Mrs. Givens. "Did you bring the aspirin?"

With a stricken expression, the housekeeper turned and clattered down the stairs. Noah, too, had disappeared, but Celia didn't have time to think of either of them. She was too terrified for the life of the man before her. After turning back the covers, she placed her ear against Cameron's chest. His lungs sounded clear, so perhaps he didn't have pneumonia. What she needed was a broad-spectrum antibiotic, but even if she could convince Noah to go in search of one, he'd have little success without a prescription.

Perspiration already soaked the sheets where Cameron lay, and a thin stream of blood trickled from his nose. He pulled himself up weakly on his elbows, then retched with dry heaves into the bucket she'd set beside the bed. Celia wiped his mouth with a damp cloth and tucked the blankets around him once again.

"Get out of here, Celia," he muttered in a voice

so weak she had to lean toward him to hear it. "If I'm contagious—"

"Shh, just go to sleep."

She pushed his damp hair back from his forehead, noting again the jagged white scar at his hairline. She bathed his face and hands with cool water and wished for ice.

"My head, the pain—" His words ended in a quiet moan, and his suffering stabbed at her heart.

"Aspirin will help. Mrs. Givens is bringing it."

His face, as white as his pillow, contorted with pain, and nausea racked his body. Cameron's survival was in her hands, and she wished for a hospital with doctors and pharmacies, but as intransigent as Mrs. Givens and Noah had been about sending for help, she might as well have wished for the moon.

For the next three days and nights, Celia didn't know if Cameron would live or die. He remained unaware of what was happening to him and around him, his body blazed with fever, and he seemed to hang precariously between life and death. She couldn't leave his side. Oblivious to the passage of time and the vagaries of the weather, she attempted to lower his fever with cool compresses. Several times a day, with Mrs. Givens's help, she changed his sweat-soaked sheets and ladled into him aspirin mixed in fruit juice laced with salt and sugar, her own version of Gatorade, to fight against the fever and dehydration.

And she prayed as she'd never prayed before.

On the second day, in an attempt to make him

cooler and more comfortable, she took Mrs. Givens's dress shears and cut his hair, tangled and matted from perspiration, trimming it close to his scalp. Noah lifted Cameron's head and shoulders while she cut. When she pulled from under him the towel that had caught the severed locks of golden hair, she slipped one of the curls into the pocket of her skirt before handing the towel to Noah to dispose of the clippings. She told herself it was a remembrance to take with her when she left the island and tried not to think that the lock might be all she'd have left of Cameron if the fever claimed him.

He didn't lose consciousness again, but remained too ill to care what was done to him.

Noah shook his head at the close-cropped hair lying against the pillow. "If Mr. Alex lives, you gonna have a lot of explaining to do."

"If he survives, I'll be happy to try."

"What you reckon he's got, Miss Celia?"

"Whatever it is, it's bad." She fought back tears, afraid if she began crying, she couldn't stop.

Noah left, and Celia remained at her vigil, catching only the briefest of catnaps in the chair beside his bed, afraid to sleep at all lest he stop breathing while she slumbered.

Cameron slept uneasily, often muttering in his sleep. She was dozing after cutting his hair, when his voice woke her.

"I love you." His words were slurred, and she could barely understand them.

"I will love you forever." He thrashed his head from side to side, as if in pain.

Celia leaned over him, but his eyes were closed, and he was dreaming. She smoothed his pillow and placed a fresh compress on his forehead.

Whipping his head back and forth upon the pillow, he sent the compress flying. "Clarissa, no!"

Had he had the strength, his voice would have screamed the words, but in his weakened state, his strongest effort produced only a guttural groan.

Disheartened, Celia returned to her chair, wondering how she could compete with a ghost for his affection. Cameron had claimed that he loved her, but Clarissa had been dead for eight years. If he still loved his wife so completely that he called for her in his suffering, what stock could Celia place in his claim of love for her?

"Don't leave me!"

"I'm here, Cameron."

But she didn't know if he called to Clarissa or her.

The third day dawned, his body still burned with fever, and he couldn't keep down the liquids Celia fed him by the spoonful. She despaired for his survival, questioning how a strong man like Cameron could endure, for he seemed to shrivel before her, his once powerful body only a slight mound beneath the covers. His formerly tanned skin stretched tight and pale like a death's head over his high cheekbones, and his breath came in tortured gasps.

In desperation, Celia doubled the aspirin dosage,

stripped the covers off his naked form, and stood for hours, cooling him with a large fan Noah had woven from palmetto leaves. She was ready to do battle with God himself to keep Cameron alive.

The fever finally broke.

Well-acquainted with every square inch, every beloved muscle and curve of him, she bathed him and tugged a soft linen nightshirt over him. For the first time in days, the grip of fear lessened on her heart. He seemed better, but terribly weak. After replacing his sheets with fresh ones, she turned the lamp low in the dresser. She left Noah with him and went downstairs for her first meal in three days.

When Celia entered the kitchen, Mrs. Givens glanced up with fear in her eyes, as if expecting the worst.

"I think he's going to be all right," Celia said.

"Praise God," the housekeeper said with a sob, not attempting to hide her tears of relief. "I feared he would die for certain."

Mrs. Givens scrubbed tears from her cheeks with the back of her hand and filled Celia a plate from dishes warming on the stove.

She managed only a few bites of the delicious fish stew before fatigue overcame her, and she laid her head on the table.

"Get yourself up to bed," Mrs. Givens ordered. "I'll sit the night with Mr. Alexander. You haven't slept for days."

Celia was too exhausted to argue. She stumbled up

the stairs, checked to see that Cameron was sleeping peacefully, then, fully clothed, fell across the bed in her own room.

CELIA AWOKE TO THE CRIES of seagulls. After a quick wash and a change of clothes, she went next door to find Cameron propped against a bank of pillows with Noah shaving the four-day stubble from his pale face.

His forehead was cool when she laid her wrist against it, but before she could pull away, he grasped her hand and placed his lips against her wrist.

The tender gesture caught her by surprise, and her heart soared with hope that Cameron had changed his mind about sending her away. "You're feeling better?"

"Thanks to you." His gaze held a warmth that seeped inside her like a blessing. "Noah told me you watched over me for three solid days."

"It was the least I could do. You took me into your home when I was shipwrecked."

"But sheltering you didn't place my life in danger. You took a great risk in caring for me. You may have caught whatever I had." He studied her with a worried gaze, as if searching for signs of illness.

"I'm fine." The emotion in his eyes made her long to tell him how much she loved him, but she remembered his last words to her before his illness, his insistence that she leave Solitaire. Cameron's life had been spared, but her future remained a question.

"You must be hungry," she said. "I'll bring you a tray."

In the kitchen, Mrs. Givens was preparing Cameron's breakfast. She looked up at Celia's arrival, her eyes swimming with tears. "I can't thank you enough for the care you've given Mr. Alexander."

"We're lucky Noah found Cameron when he did and brought him home—"

Celia's voice broke. She thought of Solitaire as home and of Noah and Mrs. Givens as the only family she had. As for Cameron, she considered him the other half of herself and didn't want to face the prospect of life without him.

Minutes later, her emotions more composed, she carried up a tray with broth, dry toast and weak tea.

Noah was putting away the shaving cup and razor. "He's all yours, Miss Celia."

Noah left, and Celia placed the tray across Cameron's lap. While he ate, she related the story of how Noah had found him and brought him home. She took comfort in the intimacy of the moment with Cameron, weak but mending, sharing with her the details of the household over breakfast.

When he finished, she removed the tray, plumped his pillows and smoothed his covers. Before she could move away, he reached for her hands and pulled her down beside him on the bed.

"I've been thinking of you ever since I awoke this morning," he said, "and of the wonderful care you've given me."

She ran her fingers across the ragged tufts of his hair. Her clumsy attempts at a haircut and his lack of color made him look like a punk rocker.

"I love you, Cameron. If you had died of fever—"

He placed his fingers against her lips. "You mustn't speak of loving me. What I have to say is difficult enough already."

A look of terrible desolation filled his eyes, and she knew what he was going to say. Knowing what was coming, however, didn't diminish the pain.

"As soon as I am strong enough," he said, "I'll sail you to Key West as I promised."

Chapter Nine

Cameron knew how close he'd come to dying and doubted he'd have survived without Celia's devoted care. With a rueful smile, he ran his fingers over his shorn head. She'd stopped at nothing in her attempts to keep him comfortable, even whacking off his hair. After the initial shock of seeing himself in the mirror and shrugging off comparisons to Billy Idol, he had to admit he liked the look and feel of his new haircut. He'd assured her he appreciated her efforts.

The depth of her feeling for him—matching his own—made sticking to his decision to take her to Key West all the harder. But it had to be done. He had no choice. If she loved him as she professed, she would keep his location secret, thus insuring his safety. And her removal from the island and his presence would guarantee her own.

She had pleaded again to stay, but he had held firm. The confused look in her eyes told him she couldn't reconcile his declaration of love for her with his decision to send her away, but he couldn't explain. If she knew his secrets, her love might turn to loathing, an attitude he couldn't face. Losing her was torment enough.

Before he could undertake the trip to Key West, however, he had to regain his strength. His weakened state reinforced how close he'd come to dying. He didn't know what he'd contracted—encephalitis, yellow or dengue fever, malaria or some virulent strain of flu—but he watched Celia closely, fearful she might develop symptoms of the disease he'd had. As time passed and she remained healthy, his worries receded, and his days were filled with bittersweet happiness at the knowledge that they'd be the last he'd spend with her.

As if sharing his wish to wring every moment of happiness from the little time they had left together, Celia was at his side every waking moment, reading aloud to him until he was strong enough to leave his bed. She supported him when he took his first wobbly steps to the veranda, where they sat and watched the everchanging face of the gulf and sky. The next day, they walked downstairs, and the day after that, as far as the dunes.

His strength grew each day, and by the fourth day, they walked to the beach, where Noah had constructed a Seminole *chickee* of cypress poles and palm fronds to protect them from the sun. Noah spread a rug across the sand beneath the shade and brought chairs and a table from the house, creating an outdoor living room.

Although the pace of their days was languid and peaceful, for Cameron they passed in a fast forward mode, rushing him nearer to the day of Celia's departure. Ten days after his fever had broken, in the late afternoon he sat in his large armchair with his feet on a hassock. During the first days of his recovery, he'd dozed often, but as his strength rallied, he'd read and made notations in his journal or at times simply smoked his pipe and gazed at the shifting seascape. No matter what he did, he was constantly aware of Celia at his side. He reveled in the melodic lilt of her voice when she read to him, the brilliance of her smile, and the special scent of her carried on the breeze.

That afternoon, she sat with her head uncovered, her magnificent auburn hair ruffled by the wind, her tanned bare feet thrust before her, and she managed to look elegant and delectable even in Mrs. Givens's oversize hand-me-downs.

"After living in London, coming here must have taken quite an adjustment," she said.

He puffed on his pipe and watched a great blue heron fly along the surf. As always, when he spoke of the past, he chose his words carefully lest he divulge too much. "From the day my father died, my life was a headlong rush of activity. I had to learn the mining business as I was running it, and the operation of the farms and other interests as well. I'd rise at four o'clock each morning, leave for the office, and often not return until midnight."

"But you were such a young man. What did you do for fun?"

"There was no fun. I hated the mines and the office, but I had an overwhelming desire to please my father—even though he was long dead—by managing the business as he would have.''

''Leaving all that behind must have lifted a terrible burden from your shoulders.''

''Only an exchange.''

''An exchange?''

''Of one burden for another.''

She paused, as if waiting for him to explain what burden he had accepted in fleeing to his island, but he couldn't divulge more.

''At least it's peaceful here,'' she finally said, ''away from the bustle of the city and the pressures of your office.''

He wondered if the misery he felt showed. ''Peace comes from the heart. I have no peace.''

Her gaze searched his face, but he could offer no further explanation.

Unable to withstand her empathetic scrutiny, he turned his attention back to the water. He looked up and down the beach, but could find no sign of the pelicans, herons and gulls that usually flocked toward the shore as the sun began to set. ''That's odd. The birds have disappeared.''

The cloudless sky appeared bleached white by the sun, and a strange stillness filled the air. He shivered with foreboding.

''Mr. Alex!'' Noah ran toward them from the dunes. ''Barometer's dropping like a dead man. Hurricane's coming!''

Cameron leaped to his feet and motioned to Noah.

"Help me carry this furniture inside. Then we can batten down the shutters."

"A hurricane?" Celia asked. "How can you be sure?"

"Noah's worked these waters all his life. He knows the signs."

"How bad will it be?" she asked.

He wished he could answer, but he had no clue whether the approaching storm was a Category One or Five, whether it would bear down on them with a storm surge from the gulf or rip across the state from the Atlantic. He had heard about the devastation Hurricane Andrew wrought on South Florida over a decade earlier and wondered if any of them would survive such a storm on the fragile barrier island.

Mrs. Givens and Celia moved furniture off the veranda, carried in extra water from the cistern, and stripped the ripe vegetables and fruit from the garden for drying and canning after the storm passed. Cameron and Noah secured the boats and fastened shutters over the windows and doors of Noah's cottage and the main house.

The wind picked up before they finished and sent dead palm fronds cartwheeling down the beach and stripped sand from the dunes. Palms bowed before the gale as darkness closed in on the island.

"Will you stay with us?" Cameron asked Noah.

The handyman shook his head. "I'll be fine at my place. I need to keep an eye on things there."

Cameron watched him leave, aware that if Noah's

cottage fell to the winds, the big house would probably perish, too.

Mrs. Givens served a cold supper in the dining
room. She had brought supplies from the kitchen before Cameron had secured the shutters. No one would
risk the open passage between the house and the
kitchen again until the storm had passed.

After supper, with Celia and Mrs. Givens, Cameron
settled in the living room to wait. The air hung hot
and heavy with moisture in the enclosed house, and
while Mrs. Givens expressed a yearning for a cup of
tea, the added heat of a fire would have been intol-
erable.

Cameron sat on the sofa and sipped a brandy,
avoiding the portrait of Clarissa and Randolph illuminated by the lamp on the mantel. Mrs. Givens
picked up sewing from her basket, and Celia flipped
through the pages of a months' old magazine. Everyone was too jittery to concentrate on anything but the
gathering force of the wind outside.

The first blast of rain shook the house, and the tu-
mult of the downpour joined the roar of the gale,
making it impossible to hear anyone speak. Wind-
driven rain oozed in under the doorways, and Cameron, with Celia's help, scurried to move furniture and
roll the oriental carpet out of harm's way.

The case clock on the mantel struck ten o'clock,
but Cameron could barely hear the chimes above the
screaming gusts that buffeted the house and shook the
shutters until he feared they would tear loose and fly

away. A crash and breaking glass sounded upstairs, and Mrs. Givens rose as if to check the source.

"Leave it," Cameron shouted and waved her back into her seat.

Across the room, Celia turned pale as the storm increased in ferocity, and Cameron recalled her earlier panic attack during a thunderstorm, spurred, no doubt, by memories of the storm that had shipwrecked her boat and almost killed her. He crossed the room, took her hand, and led her back to the sofa. After drawing her down beside him, he curved his arm around her shoulders, flashed her a smile, and gave her what he hoped was a reassuring squeeze.

Her look of gratitude almost undid him, and he was thankful for Mrs. Givens presence in the room to restrain him from following his instincts.

In another hour, the howling diminished and the shutters stopped rattling like a freight train barreling through. He could feel Celia's tension ease.

"Well, that's that." Mrs. Givens stood, shook out her skirt, and folded her sewing away. "I'll check the kitchen and make a cup of tea before bed."

"Wait," Cameron warned. "We might be in the eye."

"Eye?" the woman asked.

"Hurricanes have a center of dead calm," he explained. "If you venture out while it's passing over, you might be caught in the other half of the storm."

"Cameron's right," Celia said. "Please wait until we're certain the storm has passed completely."

The housekeeper resumed her seat and her sewing,

wiggling impatiently as the calm lengthened in the darkness outside the house. When the clock chimed midnight, she set down her handwork.

"I have to have a cup of tea." She stared at them as if daring them to contradict her.

At that moment, a wall of wind struck the house with such force, the building shook on its pilings. Mrs. Givens sat down quickly, her thirst apparently forgotten.

Cameron rose and poured everyone a snifter of brandy and passed them around. "To ease the waiting."

Celia sipped hers, and he noted with a pang of sympathy how violently her hands shook. He longed to comfort her, but restrained himself. Once the storm had passed, they would be saying goodbye. Giving in to his desires would only make that parting more difficult.

The storm continued, and the structure of the house seemed to come alive, as if it breathed. Cameron could feel the straining of the walls, the pressure of the winds, and the lifting of the eaves, as if the roof were preparing to peel away. Above the shrieking of the wind, the sharp report of objects slamming into the house jolted them, but they were prisoners of the storm, caught in the fury of the tempest, unable to do anything but wait.

The brandy must have made Celia drowsy, because in spite of her obvious jitters, she fell asleep on Cameron's shoulder. He sat without moving, unwilling to awaken her, reveling in her closeness.

WHEN CELIA AWOKE, gray daylight filtered through the shutters, and Cameron and Mrs. Givens were gone. She found them upstairs in the room across from hers, inspecting a rafter from the henhouse that the storm had pitched through the roof like a javelin. Wind-driven rain soaked the furnishings.

"It's all ruined." Mrs. Givens's chin quivered when she spoke.

"These things can be replaced," Cameron said. "We're lucky the wind didn't rip the roof from over our heads."

The rain and gray skies gradually gave way to a brilliant Florida day, and Noah joined Celia and Cameron outside, herding the cow back in its shed, which lost only a portion of its roof, taking down shutters, clearing debris, gathering the scattered hens back into their coop and staking the battered plants of the garden.

The storm had approached from the east, sparing the island the devastation of a storm surge. Inches of fresh rain filled the cistern, and aside from the damage to the henhouse and the upstairs room, Solitaire had come through the hurricane relatively unscathed.

After a day of rigorous work and the lack of sleep the night before, Celia fell into bed exhausted that night, but the hurricane had unbound memories she had worked hard to leash.

She dreamed of sailing her boat into the gulf off Clearwater Beach as she'd done when fleeing from marrying Darren. The sky sparkled clear and blue with only the sheerest wisps of cirrus above her. The brisk wind drove her craft swiftly through the calm waters, out of sight of land. She felt the exhilaration of freedom—freedom from the disastrous marriage she'd almost made.

The first hint of trouble was the strange green light dancing on the mast and lines, like the errant strikes of an electrical storm. Then the sea heaved and boiled around her, whirling in a maelstrom of green that reached into the sky, and she couldn't tell where the water ended and the ominous dark clouds, glowing neon green, began. The boat spun wildly out of control, and she grasped the side, hanging on with all her might to prevent the centrifugal force from flinging her into the green darkness. The boat rotated faster and faster, and when she could hold on no longer, she screamed, certain she was going to drown.

"Celia, wake up!" Suddenly Cameron was beside her, crushing her to his bare chest.

"The storm—"

"Shh." He brushed her hair from her face and rocked her in his arms. "It was just a dream."

She realized she was no longer dreaming, but safe in her room on Solitaire with Cameron beside her on the bed. He lifted her in his arms, carried her to the chair, and sat with her on his lap, rocking her like a baby and whispering comforting assurances in her ear.

"Tell me about it," he said.

In the darkness of the tropical night, she faced the terror that had almost killed her and relived the ordeal of the storm, describing in precise detail every bit of the experience, dragging it all from her memory, hoping to purge it forever with the telling. At times her voice wavered, and tears slid down her cheeks, but Cameron gripped her tighter, and she forged ahead. When she finished, he cupped her face in his hands and pulled her toward him.

"My God, Celia, how can I let you go?" His words erupted in a guttural groan, and his lips crushed hers.

She spun again into a maelstrom, not of darkness and terror and cold green light, but a whirlpool of heat and passion that started at the core of her being and radiated outward. Aware with every fiber of her being of his body pressed against hers, she returned his kiss with a fervor she'd never known.

When the kiss ended, she gasped for air and answered his question. "You can't send me away. I belong to you for all time."

"I should have taken you to Key West while I had the strength, before the fever—"

His mouth claimed hers again, and her body melded to his. She splayed her hands across the broad expanse of his warm, bare chest where his heart beat with an insistent primal rhythm. With tender urgency, he tugged the nightgown over her head and pushed her back on the bed beneath him. The heat in his gaze simmered in the moonlight.

"You are so beautiful." His words echoed like a prayer.

She opened her arms to him, and he hastily stripped away his clothes, standing tall and golden before her as she remembered him from his morning swim.

He covered her with his warmth, his lips grazed her throat, her breasts, and his hands trailed reverently over her body, causing shivers of delight.

"I never knew love could feel like this," she said, struggling for breath against the delicious sensations.

"I want you, Celia, but—"

She pressed her fingers against his lips. "No *buts,* no regrets."

With a groan of surrender, he kissed her again, and she opened her mouth to his, mingling their breaths, tasting the essence of him. Her heart pounded like the surf on the beach, and she arched beneath him. He positioned himself above her and with forceful gentleness, drove his body into hers.

She cried out with pleasure and clasped him closer, oblivious to everything but the pulsing thrust that joined them together in a bond as old as time. With eyes wide open, she feasted on his face, memorizing every detail of him against the time when she might have to leave. Caught in the blaze of passion, she still registered the glow of moonlight that surrounded them, the kiss of the tropical breeze, the weight of his body on hers, the rich, masculine scent of him, the smoothness of the sheets against her back, but most of all, the powerful, riveting plunge that shattered solitude and isolation. She savored it all, capturing the feelings and images to last a lifetime, if need be.

Fiercely, tenderly, he cried her name, and it reverberated in the midnight darkness. In an explosion of sensation, she tumbled over the edge into a star-studded oblivion where nothing existed but the two of them.

After a moment, Cameron slid next to her and drew her against him. She nestled happily in his embrace, sated and content.

''I love you, Celia.'' His breath caressed her ear. ''Marry me.''

Chapter Ten

With happiness coursing through her, Celia sat up and stared at him. "You're serious?"

"I've never been more serious in my life."

Cameron's response stunned her into silence. She wanted nothing more in the world than to remain on Solitaire with him, but his mercurial personality left her curious, wondering why he'd undergone yet another change of heart.

"Would you rather I take you to Key West?" he asked.

She could hear the disappointment in his voice, but a cloud obscuring the moon kept her from seeing his face clearly.

"No! Please don't send me away."

He grasped her shoulders, then slid his hands down the length of her arms. She responded to his touch with a shiver of pleasure, an echo of the intimacy they'd just shared.

"If you remain on Solitaire," he said, "it must be because you love me. I couldn't bear having you here if you didn't return my love."

She lifted her lips to his once more, then after a long moment, pulled away. She would, she assured herself, learn to live with his changing moods. "I do love you, Cameron, and I will marry you, as soon as you wish."

He pulled her down beside him, sculpting his body to hers like nesting spoons. "Sleep well, Celia. We have much to do tomorrow."

In the warm shelter of his arms, she fell instantly asleep.

Had she known what the future held for her, she wouldn't have slept at all.

"WHO'D HAVE THOUGHT? A wedding on Solitaire." Mrs. Givens beamed her approval when Cameron announced their plans at breakfast. She placed the last of the hot dishes on the sideboard and left them alone in the dining room to complete their plans.

Celia gazed out at the perfect day. The morning, like her heart, was filled with sunshine. A mockingbird's song floated in on the clear, cool air, and the gentle breeze, laden with the smells of saltwater, ruffled the curtains.

She gazed across the table at Cameron, thinking how she would begin each day for the rest of her life having breakfast with him. His hair was growing back, and he'd lost his punk rocker aura.

"Cameron—"

"Yes."

"I was just thinking how little you know about me. How can you be sure you want to marry me?"

His smiled melted her heart. "I know you are beautiful and intelligent, compassionate and brave. What more could any man wish for in a wife?"

"A sense of humor?"

He looked startled for a moment, then laughed. "That, too."

"Did Clarissa have a sense of humor?"

The dry toast crumbled in his hand. "I won't speak of her."

"But if I'm to be your wife—"

"You are unlike Clarissa in every way, and I love you for it. Let the matter rest at that."

The severity of his tone ended any further discussion, but Celia hoped that Cameron would come to trust her more. She willingly dropped the topic of Clarissa for the subject that was foremost on her mind.

"How can we be married here, without a minister or notary or justice of the peace?"

He grasped her hand and kissed her palm. "We'll proclaim our own vows."

"But will that be legal?"

"I'll prepare papers for us to sign and be witnessed by Mrs. Givens and Noah."

"Why don't we just sail to Key West and be married there?"

Cameron set his teacup down carefully and wiped his mouth with his napkin before he spoke. Celia had the feeling he was playing for time.

"Since you are remaining on the island, there is no

need for us to appear in Key West and advertise our presence here.''

"Very well." In her lovestruck state, Celia would have agreed to almost anything. "We'll be married here. But when?"

"Next week."

She was surprised at the delay. He had seemed so anxious for them to be married immediately. She loved the man, but she understood him hardly at all.

"There's much to prepare," he explained.

"Like what?"

"First, we must locate our vows in *The Book of Common Prayer* in my study and learn them."

Celia couldn't see why memorizing a wedding ceremony would take a week. Cameron must have read her questioning expression, because he rose from his chair and stood behind hers with his hands on her shoulders.

"Dearest Celia, just because we don't have a church to be married in doesn't mean that you shouldn't have the grand wedding to which you're entitled."

She remembered the small but elegant ceremony planned for her wedding with Darren and shuddered. "But I don't want a grand—"

He leaned forward and pressed his lips to hers, stifling her protest. "The sky will be your cathedral and the sounds of the waves your orchestra. We'll be married on the beach at sunset."

She turned and pulled him into her arms. "I love you."

Again he smiled, erasing any doubts she'd felt about the legality of their marriage.

"Mrs. Givens," he said, "will prepare us a wedding feast. We can serve it under the *chickee* on the beach after the ceremony."

"The hurricane blew it down, remember?"

"Then we'll ask Noah to build us another one."

He tugged her from her chair, lifted her off her feet, and whirled her around the room. Then he set her down and kissed her long and hard, until the room whirled while she stood still.

"I never believed I could be a happy man. You have given me hope."

Whistling, he went off to his study to find the prayer book, and Celia carried the breakfast dishes out to the kitchen.

"I'm so happy, m'dear, for both of you."

Celia couldn't tell if the redness in Mrs. Givens's eyes was the result of tears or her proximity to the smoking woodstove. She explained to the housekeeper about their plans for the wedding, and if Mrs. Givens considered the ceremony unorthodox, she kept her opinion to herself.

On the subject of the wedding dinner, she offered her enthusiastic support. "I'll bake you a wedding cake the likes of which you've never seen. But what will you wear?"

"The blue dress—"

"Good heavens, no! Mr. Alexander has seen you in that dress."

"You're not superstitious?"

"Indeed I am! It's terribly bad luck for a man to see his bride in her bridal clothes before the ceremony. The yellow dress is almost finished. We'll add a special touch or two."

Although Celia was amused by the housekeeper's fears, she agreed with her choice of a dress. The color was a pale yellow, more the shade of heavy cream. With the inset of ivory lace at the neckline that Mrs. Givens suggested, it would be a perfect wedding dress—nothing like the Vera Wang creation she'd bought for her marriage to Darren, but then Cameron was nothing like Darren.

Then another thought struck Celia and she laughed aloud as she pictured herself in her wedding dress—and sneakers.

"What is it?" Mrs. Givens asked.

"Shoes. I only have the one pair—and not very bridal ones at that."

"Noah has some hides he's tanned. They're in the cowshed. I can cut soles from them and make you slippers out of some ivory satin I have."

"Mrs. Givens, you are amazing."

While Celia did the washing up, Mrs. Givens prepared bread dough for a week's baking. Celia's thoughts were happy, focused on her approaching marriage, but her mind kept returning to Clarissa, as a tongue seeks out an aching tooth.

"Were you there when Cameron married Clarissa?" Celia asked, "and please don't tell me you can't speak of her. If I'm marrying Cameron, I should know about his past."

"What Mr. Alexander chooses to tell you is his business."

"I'm not asking you to divulge any secrets. Just tell me, as one woman to another, what their wedding was like."

Mrs. Givens scratched her nose as she remembered, leaving a smear of flour across its tip. "It was the most magnificent wedding of its day. Married in St. Paul's, they were, with half of London there to see."

"And Clarissa's dress?"

"All silk and tulle, and yards and yards of Brussels lace, even her veil."

"All white?"

"Oh, no. All in a lovely shade of silvery gray that set off her dark eyes and her complexion—like the finest white porcelain, it was. You can see it in her portrait."

"And Cameron?"

"Dressed like a lord, all the way to his fine silk hat."

"They must have been very happy."

Mrs. Givens pummeled the dough on the table before her angrily, and when she glanced up at Celia, her eyes were blazing. "They were the two most miserable people on God's earth."

The housekeeper's statement shocked Celia, shattering the picture she'd had of Cameron and Clarissa. "But it was their wedding day."

Mrs. Givens wiped her floured hands on her apron and gazed at Celia with sad eyes. "The two hardly knew one another. Clarissa's father was a business partner of Mr. Alexander, and he was desperately ill. He wanted a husband for his daughter before he died.''

"And Cameron, what did he want?"

"To protect his investments by marrying the other half of them."

The cold, calculated arrangement sickened Celia. "Even though they started out unhappily, surely they must have grown to love one another over time?"

The housekeeper crossed the kitchen and placed her hand on Celia's arm. "One of the reasons I'm so very happy about your marriage, m'dear, is that it offers Cameron the first chance for true happiness he's ever had. Let it go at that. Don't muddy the waters with too many questions."

Cameron called Celia into the house then, and in the flurry of preparations over the next week, she forgot Mrs. Givens's account of Cameron's marriage to Clarissa.

Until it was too late.

THE MORNING OF HER wedding day dawned overcast and drizzly, and, sensitized to omens by Mrs. Givens's superstitious nature, Celia pondered the significance of the weather. But as the day progressed, the sky cleared, and the sun shone with enough radiance to please any bride.

Noah journeyed inland during the rainy morning and returned with an armload of goldenrod, wild orchids and lacy ferns, which Mrs. Givens fashioned into a huge bouquet tied with ivory satin lovers' knots.

The three-tiered cake stood ready on the kitchen table, rich buttery layers with a filling of raisins, nuts, and dates in between, all covered with a creamy icing decorated with glistening orange leaves and blossoms of yellow frangipani.

"If you'd wait a few months, we'd have orange blossoms," Mrs. Givens teased as she placed the fresh flowers on the cake.

Late in the afternoon, Celia bathed in the copper tub, twisted her hair into a French braid, intertwined with ivory ribbons and frangipani blossoms. She slipped on her dress and surveyed herself in the full-length mirror.

A wide-eyed stranger stared back at her. "I hope you know what you're doing this time," the stranger said.

Celia thought of her late parents and wished they could be here for her wedding. Even more than the average bride, she was beginning an entirely new life, joining Cameron willingly—even joyfully—in his exile on Solitaire. She couldn't go home again, but she would make the island her home, and home for the man who had been so unhappy when she first arrived. She slid her feet into the delicate satin slippers Mrs. Givens had made and went to meet her groom.

On the beach, Mrs. Givens, in her best dress of violet silk, stood proudly by the table beneath the *chickee*. Centered with the massive cake and decorated with tropical flowers, greenery and candles shielded from the wind by hurricane globes, the table, filled with an amazing variety of dishes, looked like a buffet on a cruise ship. The only thing missing was an ice sculpture.

Mrs. Givens and Noah applauded as Celia stepped onto the path between the dunes.

Cameron came forward and offered his arm. Dressed simply in a linen shirt and fitted slacks tucked into his high, polished boots, he looked more handsome than ever, and her heart swelled with pride that this fascinating and complex man loved her.

Together they walked to the water's edge and gazed westward toward the huge orb of gold hanging just above the horizon. Joining hands, they gazed into one another's eyes and recited the vows they had memorized.

Cameron placed a gold ring set with a sparkling square-cut emerald on her finger. "My father gave this ring to my mother when I was born. The emerald is my birthstone."

She caught the glint of tears in his eyes before he kissed her. As they broke from their embrace, the sun slipped beneath the horizon, and an incredible flash of green burst forth from its exit point and bathed the sky in pale green light.

"An omen," Mrs. Givens said.

"A sign of my good fortune." Cameron kissed Celia again. "Mrs. Alexander, you have made me the luckiest and happiest of men."

Celia, too, in the joy of the moment, considered the flash of green a symbol of good luck.

THE WEEKS FOLLOWING her wedding were the happiest Celia had ever known. As had been his habit, Cameron rose before dawn for his plunge in the gulf, and an hour later, when she joined him at breakfast, she always found some small gift or token waiting beside her plate. While other women might have yearned for expensive jewelry and hothouse flowers, she delighted in his simple gifts, seeing in them Cameron's way of showing his love for her.

The first morning, she discovered a magnificent conch shell, its shining pink interior scrubbed clean.

"It's beautiful." She ran her hand across its knurled surface. "I'll make a display of the shells I've collected, and this will be the focal point."

"So long as you keep it close at hand," Cameron said.

"Why? If you wanted me to wear it next to my heart, it should have been smaller."

"Let me show you." He picked up the huge shell, placed one end to his lips, and blew.

The trumpeting blast brought Mrs. Givens on the run from the kitchen.

"God in heaven, I thought it was the call of Judgment Day," she said before returning to her tasks.

"You see its effectiveness," Cameron told Celia with a grin. "If you need me, just sound a few blasts on this."

Other mornings there were wildflowers, exotic shells, a gull's feather, a piece of driftwood carved like a dolphin and a book of poems marked at a special place.

"Cameron, you spoil me. I love your surprises, but I have nothing to give you in return."

"Nothing? Dearest Celia, you have given me back my life."

While his statement may have sounded melodramatic, Celia noted evidence of new vitality in Cameron every day. His step seemed lighter, he laughed often, and he had abandoned his habit of consuming several snifters of brandy in order to sleep.

He planned every day like an adventure, beginning the day after the wedding.

"Every bride should have a wedding journey." He returned the conch shell to her and attacked his breakfast with enthusiasm.

"A journey? To Key West? Or back to England?"

"I will never return there." His words fell flat and cold on her ears.

"I'm sorry. I thought—"

"We will have to amuse ourselves with day trips. Today I'll show you the dry prairies inland."

"Where Noah cuts grass for the cow?"

"It's more than grass. It—I can't describe it. You must see it for yourself."

"I'd love to see it, but—"

"If you don't wish to go, say so." Cameron set down his knife and fork. "I only want what pleases you."

"I *want* to see it, but I don't have suitable clothes for tromping through a prairie."

Cameron grinned. "We'll take care of that."

Later, outfitted in one of Cameron's shirts and a

pair of his slacks, cinched at the waist with a belt and rolled at the ankles, Celia joined him at the pier. They set sail for the mainland, and she snuggled into the curve of his arm as he sat at the tiller.

"I've been thinking of a suggestion you made." His amber eyes sparkled with excitement, making him even more attractive than usual. "The idea of writing a book about the Ten Thousand Islands is very appealing. And to maintain my anonymity, I can use a pseudonym."

"It's a big undertaking."

"Not if you'll help me." He squeezed her shoulder gently and favored her with a loving glance. "We'll work as a team, observing and taking notes."

Celia smiled her approval, drinking in the sight of him against the cloudless sky with the sun glinting off his hair. He pulled her closer and kissed her, until the wind shifted, drawing his attention back to his sailing.

"At this rate," she teased, "writing that book may take a very long time."

"We have all the time in the world."

All that day and the weeks after, Celia slogged with Cameron through wet prairies, sawgrass, swamp lilies and cattails, noting pickerel weed ponds, alligator flag and potato marshes filled with herons, limpkins, egrets, ibis, wood storks and sandhill cranes. Cameron pointed out marsh pinks and grass pinks, false foxglove and coreopsis that would flood new green grasses with color in the spring. Together they clipped samples of the vegetation and sketched the birds, detailing colors and markings as well as nesting grounds and feeding habits.

Life in the outdoors agreed with Celia, and she reveled in the fresh air. Most of all, she delighted in Cameron's company.

In the evenings after dinner, they tabulated their findings, pressed samples of grasses and blossoms into the books in Cameron's study and discussed the best methods of organizing the information they'd gathered.

Afterward, before bedtime, they'd take a blanket to the beach and lie on their backs for hours, watching the stars, easily picking out Orion's Belt, the Big and Little Dippers, and the North Star.

One night, a group of meteors streaked across the velvet darkness above them—myriad shooting stars. Celia made a wish that she would always be as happy with Cameron beside her as she was that moment. As if reading her thoughts, he drew her into his arms and made love to her on the soft sand. She fell asleep in his arms, and when she awakened, dawn lit the eastern sky. Cameron was wading into the gulf for his morning swim. She removed her clothes and joined him, wondering if Adam and Eve had been as happy in Eden, and if so, what horrible punishment their banishment had been.

"I promised Mrs. Givens I'd go fishing for her today." Cameron had lain on the blanket until the breeze dried his skin and was pulling on his clothes. "Want to go with me?"

The November day had turned hot and muggy, and

the prospect of spending hours on the open water in the hot sun had no appeal for Celia. "Would you mind terribly if I didn't?"

He tugged her to her feet and kissed her while she struggled to cover her nakedness with her discarded clothes. "Not at all. I don't relish the outing myself, but we need fish, unless we want to eat beans until Captain Biggins arrives with supplies."

Later in the morning, with a sinking heart, Celia watched Cameron sail away. She hadn't been separated from him for more than a few minutes since their wedding, and she felt as if she'd lost a part of herself when his boat vanished behind a mangrove island. She crossed the vegetable garden to Noah's cottage where he sat on the front steps, weaving a fishing net.

"May I join you?"

His face split into a welcoming grin. "Morning, Miss Celia."

She sat beside him and took a raisin bun tied in a napkin from her pocket. After breaking it in two, she offered Noah half.

He shook his head. "Done had my breakfast."

She munched her late breakfast while he knotted his cord and severed it from the net with a large knife, honed razor-sharp.

"Seems like Mr. Alex ain't so lonesome now he's married." Noah regarded her with a twinkle in his soft brown eyes.

"I still don't understand why he's hidden himself away all this time."

Noah wove his cord through his net and knotted it again. "He was full of misery when he come here. I always thought rich, white men had everything and that all of them was happy. But Mr. Alex was about the miserablest man I ever did see."

"But why, Noah? Like you've said, he seems to have everything. What made him so unhappy?" Her conscience panged her only slightly at prying about her husband behind his back. After all, the better she knew him, the more she could love him as he deserved.

Noah's high forehead wrinkled in thought. "It's a puzzle, but I've had lots of time to think on it. I figure it has to do with his first wife and his son what died before he come here."

Although Celia loved Cameron unconditionally, her knowledge of his life before she met him had huge gaps. If Noah could fill them, she was more than willing to listen.

"He'd been here six years when I arrived," she said. "For a man to live with such unhappiness for so long a time—it's not rational."

"I know it don't seem likely, but he was pining for his dead kin. He told me so himself."

She felt a pang of envy that Cameron had shared with Noah what he'd refused to tell her. "What did he say?"

Noah leaned back on his elbows and stared out across the garden. "I remember it like it was yesterday. It was right after Mrs. Givens and all the furniture come. Mr. Alex called me into the parlor to help him open a crate. Inside was the picture, the one that's hanging over the fireplace now.

"When we'd pulled the last nail outta the crate, Mr. Alex lifted the picture out and leaned it against the mantel. When he looked at it the first time, he cried out—a pitiful sound, like it was dragged from the bottom of his soul."

Celia fidgeted uncomfortably at the thought of Cameron's agony and wished she could have been there to ease his pain.

"He waved his arm," Noah said, "motioning me outta the room. When I left, I could hear him sobbing all the way over here."

"He wept, but said nothing?"

Noah shook his grizzled head. "He didn't leave the parlor that whole day. Whenever I'd pass by, I could hear the brandy bottle clinking against his glass, and I knew he was trying to drown his sorrow in spirits."

"Had he always been a heavy drinker?"

"Uh-uh. He wasn't drunk once the whole time we was building these houses. The day that picture was opened was the first ever—and there ain't been one as bad since."

Celia glowed with satisfaction that Cameron hadn't taken a drink since their wedding, a comforting sign of his current happiness.

"That night," Noah said, "Mrs. Givens asked me to carry Mr. Alex up to his bed. I went into the parlor and found him sitting on the floor in front of the painting. At the time, I didn't know who they was, so I asked him. 'My wife and child,' he says, and he laughed, an awful sound. Made the hair stand up on the back of my neck.''

Noah rubbed the back of his neck as if remembering. ''I asked him if he left them in England when he come here. He answered real queer.''

''What did he say?''

''He says, 'I suppose you could say they're in England, although Mrs. Givens swears they're in heaven, wherever that is.' Then he gets this wild look in his eyes, coulda burned a hole right through me. 'They're the reason I'm here,' he says.''

Noah shivered in the noonday heat. '''But I thought you said they was dead,' I told him.''

The silence grew long as Celia waited for Noah to continue. When she could stand it no longer, she prodded him. ''What did he say then?''

Noah stared at her with wide, sad eyes. ''I'll never forget his answer. 'Oh yes, they're dead all right,' he tells me. 'I killed them.'''

Chapter Eleven

In spite of the hot Florida sun, Celia felt chilled to the bone, and a horrible darkness settled in her heart, sucking the light from the day. Had she escaped marriage with one murderer only to fall in love with another?

"Cameron couldn't have killed his wife and son," she insisted. "You must have misunderstood him."

"I heard him plain enough," Noah said, "but you're right. Mr. Alex couldn't harm nobody. It was just the liquor talking."

Wrestling with the horrible suspicion Noah had planted in her mind, Celia walked back to the house. Then guilt joined her distrust, and she castigated herself for considering for even an instant that Cameron could have murdered Clarissa and Randolph. Had Cameron been on the island, she would have confronted him with Noah's tale and begged an explanation, but he would be gone the entire day, perhaps even into the night if the fish were running, and she couldn't bear the agony of uncertainty that long.

Remembering the newspaper clippings she'd found

in his desk weeks ago and hoping to purge her suspicions, she hurried to the study. Fortunately, Cameron had left the key to the drawers on the desk surface. Her hands shook as she unlocked the top one and removed the folder of yellowed clippings from the drawer and spread them across the desktop.

What she read made her ill.

According to the various newspaper accounts, Clarissa and Randolph had been bludgeoned to death in their Devonshire mansion. Cameron, too, had been injured and found unconscious beside their bodies, his scalp almost lifted from his head by the force of a cutting blow. He had hovered near death in a hospital for weeks after the murders, and when he recovered, claimed to have no memory of the night they died.

Details of the police search for the killer revealed a cold trail with no leads or suspects. Then the articles began to raise questions about who would have had motive for such a crime. Nothing had been stolen the night of the tragedy, and no one had been found with a vendetta against the family. Gossip had begun to circulate in London that Cameron himself had murdered his wife and son in order to inherit her fortune, left by her recently deceased father. Rumormongers hinted that Clarissa had injured Cameron in her efforts to protect herself and her son. The last clipping in the file stated that the police had taken Cameron in for questioning, then released him for lack of enough evidence to prosecute.

Celia replaced the articles in their folder and shoved them into the drawer. The clippings had only

fueled her suspicions. Conflicting emotions surged
through her, a longing for Cameron to return mixed
with fear of what he might tell her. The Cameron she
knew couldn't have committed such a heinous act, but
how well did she really know the man she'd married
so hastily? Had she allowed herself to be bedazzled
by his good looks and the paradise in which he lived?
Was the secret self she'd sensed within the man she'd
married really a killer?

Unable to endure waiting for Cameron, she confronted Mrs. Givens in the kitchen.

"Hungry already?" the housekeeper asked.

"I'm too ill to eat." Celia slumped in a chair beside the stove.

"Not the fever!" Mrs. Givens hurried to feel her
forehead, but Celia brushed the woman's hand aside.

"Heartsick about Cameron. I've just read the newspaper accounts of the murders of Clarissa and Randolph. Some suggest that Cameron killed them."

A collage of emotions crossed the older woman's
face. "And what do *you* think, m'dear?"

Celia rubbed her forehead with the back of her
hand, as if trying to erase the confusion in her mind.
"My heart tells me he couldn't have, but my head—
I don't know."

Mrs. Givens went to the stove and, following her
prescription for every occasion, filled the teapot. In
maddening silence, Celia watched her pour a cup for
herself and one for Celia. When the housekeeper had
handed Celia her tea and taken the chair across from
her, Celia could stand it no longer.

"Did Cameron kill them? You must tell me."

"Only Mr. Alexander can answer that question, and you must ask him if you wish to know the truth."

"Are you telling me that you don't know?"

Mrs. Givens shrugged her plump shoulders. "I have never asked him, and he has never said. But I do know the Cameron I raised from a babe is incapable of such violence."

Celia knew the man she loved was incapable of it as well, but she wondered if the other side of Cameron, the side he had hidden from her, might be inclined to such horrors. She recalled his insistence on not leaving the island, his blocking her attempts to signal for help, his refusal to speak of Clarissa. Were those the workings of a guilt-free mind?

Then she remembered his words to her the day they had picnicked on the mangrove island: *"You must run from this place as fast as you can, flee for your life…for your own safety."*

Had he feared he might harm her as he had his wife and child?

Celia knew too little to draw reasonable conclusions.

"You must tell me what you can," she begged. "God knows, I want to believe he didn't do it."

Mrs. Givens sipped her tea and scrunched her face into a frown. "There's little enough I *can* tell. I wasn't there."

"But I thought—"

"It was my yearly holiday. From the time I first worked for the Alexanders, every year when they went down to the Devon estate, I'd spend that first week visiting my sister, God rest her soul, in Liverpool. A woman from the home farm took my place during the day, and Clarissa cared for Randolph at night."

"So the family was alone when it happened?"

"Normally the servants would have been below stairs, but there was a festival in the village that night, and Mr. Alexander had given them time off to attend. The upstairs maid discovered the bodies when she came home in time to turn down the beds."

"And nothing was stolen?"

"Not a thing. Mrs. Alexander—Clarissa was still wearing her jewelry when they found her, Mr. Alexander's wallet was full, and the house intact."

"Why would someone want to harm them? Did Cameron have enemies?" The more Celia learned, the more puzzling the whole affair became.

"Mr. Alexander was a shrewd businessman, and he had keen competitors, but he was honest and fair, so none could be identified with reason to wish him harm."

"But if someone *believed* he had cause—"

"Aye, there's always that. And there's the possibility of sick minds that simply kill for the sport of it."

"But you're speaking only of possibilities. No one was ever charged?" Celia held her breath, dreading to hear that Cameron might have run from the law.

"No one. Captain Biggins brings us the London papers, and I've watched for years to see if the killers have been caught, but nothing new has been reported.''

"And Cameron," Celia asked, "what does he say about all this?"

"Mr. Alexander doesn't speak of it, and he has requested that I not mention it to him. You are the only person who's heard the names of Clarissa and Randolph cross my lips since I set foot on this island.''

Mrs. Givens drank the last of her tea and set her cup aside. "It's as I told you, m'dear. You must ask him—but do not forget that he is the man you love and married, no matter what he tells you."

Her words were no comfort to Celia. If anything, they caused more turmoil in her heart. Everything she learned raised more questions.

"There is one thing you can tell me." Celia hesitated to ask, because she dreaded the answer. "Did Cameron love Clarissa?"

The tortured look on Mrs. Givens's face gave her answer before she spoke. "Cameron came as close to hating Clarissa as he did to hating anyone," she said with obvious reluctance.

"But why? She was his *wife*."

The housekeeper twisted her apron in her hands, an outward sign of her agitated emotions. "Cameron had never been in love. His was a marriage of convenience made to cement a business partnership."

"I can't believe that Cameron—even in his youth—would be so callous as to marry for money."

"He believed his partner. The man had been like

a father to him since his own had died. Clarissa was a beautiful woman, and her father convinced Cameron that love would grow—with time.''

''But it didn't?''

Mrs. Givens shook her head. ''Things grew worse, if anything.''

''I still don't know why.''

''That is another thing only Mr. Alexander can tell you.''

''You must have some impressions of Clarissa, besides the fact that she was beautiful.'' Celia knew that fact for herself. Clarissa's loveliness radiated from the portrait over the mantel.

''I didn't like her, but I thought I was biased, thinking no one was good enough for Mr. Alexander. Now I know better.''

''What do you mean?''

''I'm very fond of you, m'dear, and think you make him a very good wife, so it must have been Clarissa herself that I didn't approve of.'' She reached over and squeezed Celia's hand. ''You must have faith in him, and remember all things work to the good.''

Celia wished she shared the housekeeper's optimism, but she couldn't shake the feeling of disaster that enveloped her. She longed for Cameron's return, for the reassurance of his arms around her, and his explanation that would cleanse the doubts that weighed on her mind.

She refused Mrs. Givens's offer of lunch and returned to the study, where she reread every clipping, searching for some clue of exoneration but finding nothing but more doubts. Suddenly the walls of the house seemed to close in on her, and she fled to the beach to walk the length and breadth of the island as if devils pursued her. The entire time she kept watch for the first glimpse of Cameron's sail.

She paused at the site where they'd spread their blanket the night before to study the heavens, where they'd melded their bodies and their hearts in an ecstasy of passion before falling asleep in each other's arms. The images calmed her until she remembered that Cameron had joined with Clarissa in such an embrace, and Randolph had been the result.

Now both Randolph and Clarissa were dead.

Celia stripped off her clothes, wishing she could rip the suspicions from her mind as easily, and dove into the gulf. She swam to the farthest sandbar and back to shore, then out again, until she had exhausted herself with the effort. But her mind would not rest, turning over and over, examining and reexamining what had happened to Clarissa and Randolph, and trying to assess Cameron's part in all of it.

She dressed and lay down on the hot sand, buried her face in her arms, and longed for peace.

She didn't know how long she slept, but suddenly she was swept up in strong arms, and Cameron held her close.

"Good God, Celia, you gave me a scare. You looked as if you'd washed up on the beach half-dead."

She heard the anxiety in his voice and lifted her

arms to return his embrace, but all her suspicions returned in a rush, and she pushed away from him. "Set me down. I must talk with you."

He placed her on her feet and lowered his head to her neck, nuzzling her throat with his lips. "Talk? Not now. I have thought of you—and last night—all day."

"Please, don't." She jerked away and began walking up the beach.

Cameron followed her. "What's wrong?"

She turned, taking in the face and body she loved and wondering if the mind and heart they contained could have deceived her by sheltering a monster.

"Clarissa," was all she said.

She watched the blood drain from his face and his muscles go slack as he slumped to sit on the sand. "How did you find out?"

"The newspapers in your desk."

"You searched my desk?" Anger flashed in his amber eyes.

"That was wrong of me, but not as wrong as your not telling me the truth," she lashed out at him.

"The truth?"

"Did you murder her, Cameron, and your son?" Celia fell to her knees before him in the sand and watched every nuance of his expression, hoping to hear an explanation, an answer to the puzzle that had tormented her all day.

"I wish I knew the truth." Cameron's words poured forth in a groan of agony.

"How can you not know? You were there."

He clasped his head as if it ached. "But I was drunk. Falling down drunk."

The implications of his words stunned her. If Cameron didn't know the truth, there was no one who could tell her, no one to ease the torture of not knowing. "Surely you remember *something!*"

He raised his head and looked at her, and the bleakness in his eyes terrified her. "I have only one memory of the events of that night, a memory I have shared with no one. But I won't keep it from you, even though your knowing might kill the love you have for me."

Celia held her breath, and his eyes bored into hers, hypnotizing her with their pain.

"It's a strange memory, a recollection of sensation rather than a visual image." Tears filled his eyes and slid down the sharp angles of his cheekbones.

"What kind of sensation?"

"The crunch of bones beneath my knuckles. That is all I can remember."

She sank back on her heels, staring at him in horror, not knowing whether to gather him in her arms or run for her life. "You remember hitting Clarissa?"

"I remember hitting someone, but I don't know if it was Clarissa."

Cameron grasped her shoulders and pulled her toward him. "When you think of the torment you have suffered today, not knowing my guilt or innocence, compound this day by three hundred and sixty-five and that by eight years, and you'll know what I've endured, not knowing what I've done."

She tried to harden her heart against him. "But if you are guilty—"

"I deserve every moment of the torment—and more. But if I'm not?"

"How will you ever know?"

"I hope my memory of that night will someday return."

"But it's been eight years. Shouldn't you go back to London and try to prove your innocence?"

He shook his head slowly, like a wounded animal. "If there had been witnesses—besides the killer—they would have come forward by now. The police, who are trained to solve such crimes, are perplexed, so what good could I do on a trail eight years cold?"

His eyes chilled her like cold fire, and she shivered in the heat.

"There are many in London," he added, "who believe I must have done it. I don't want them convincing me, too. And there is someone who believes so strongly that I'm guilty, he's tried to take justice in his own hands. Twice before I came here, there were attempts on my life."

Celia twisted from his grasp and moved down the beach in an attempt to gather her thoughts from the conflicting emotions swirling inside her. She loved Cameron, but she knew only the man he had allowed her to see. Had he hidden a part of himself from her?

"Cameron." She turned back to him. "Don't you *know* whether you are capable of murder?"

"That is one of the puzzles I've tried to solve during my exile on this island, but I've reached no conclusions. There are too many factors.''

''Like what?''

''I had been drinking heavily earlier that evening, and people have been known to lose their reason under the influence of alcohol.''

''Alcohol releases inhibitions against natural inclinations, but I can't believe it would have made you a murderer if you weren't inclined to be one.''

He ran his hands over his close-cropped hair. ''Inclination. That is the other factor. I've spent hours reading and studying, questioning myself, trying to ascertain whether a thought is *always* the father of the deed.''

''I don't understand.''

He lifted his head and met her eyes unflinchingly. ''I *wanted* Clarissa dead.''

Celia felt as if he socked her in the stomach and all the oxygen had been drawn from the air. Mrs. Givens had said that Cameron almost hated Clarissa, but most people used hate as a relative term, spanning the spectrum from mild dislike to intense vindictiveness. ''Did you hate her enough to kill her?''

''It's a very long story, one I should have told you before I asked you to marry me.''

''Why didn't you?''

The pleading in his eyes leeched the anger from her heart. ''Because you had made me so incredibly happy, I didn't want to spoil it with talk of Clarissa. But I'll tell you everything now, if you'll hear me out.''

Celia sat on a log of driftwood half-buried in the sand, and Cameron sat in front of her with his arms clasped around his knees. The beauty of the gulf and the island sparkled around her, contrasting painfully with the agony in her heart.

"Clarissa's father, my business partner," Cameron began, "suffered from a weak heart that could have killed him at any moment. Clarissa was his only child, although he had treated me like a son since my own father died. Nothing seemed more natural than the two of us marrying, binding together our families and our families' fortunes. I was only twenty-one and had been a very sheltered young man. My business had left me little time for socializing. My mother had died when I was young, and I knew little of women or domestic life."

"You had Mrs. Givens."

"Yes, and she's stood by me through all of this, God bless her."

He gazed across the gulf toward the horizon where the sun was setting in a blaze of pink and orange, shot through with gold. Celia remembered their wedding on the beach and the flash of green at sunset.

"Clarissa and I were happy enough at first," he said. "She complained because I spent too much time at work, but that work also supplied her with ample clothes and allowances for her parties and other social activities, which were the focus of her life. I thought I was happy."

"But you weren't?"

"I never knew what true happiness was until you

came to me. Clarissa and I moved through life like two trains on parallel tracks. We shared neither interests nor friends, and our paths only crossed at mealtimes.''

''But there was Randolph.'' Celia doubted he'd been conceived during dinner.

''Poor little Randolph. He's the reason I hated his mother.'' Cameron hid his face on his folded arms, unable or unwilling to look at her.

Celia recalled the boy's keepsakes packed carefully away in the top of Cameron's closet. ''Are you saying you didn't want a son?''

He lifted his head, eyes blazing. ''Randolph was the joy of my life.''

''But—''

''It was Clarissa who didn't want him. From the day she discovered she was pregnant, she raged against him, complaining that he ruined her figure and made her feel unwell. Once he was born, she left him entirely in the care of Mrs. Givens, except when she felt compelled to play the doting mother. Then she would dress him up and parade him before her friends, but the poor child saw her as a stranger and shrank from her. His timid behavior enraged her, and she screamed at him, calling him horrible names.''

''But he was so small.'' Celia thought of the winsome, mischievous grin of the adorable boy in the portrait.

''I didn't know about the abuse until much later, and thought I'd put a stop to it. Mrs. Givens protected him when she could, but when I wasn't at home, Clarissa vented her rage on the boy. I believe she saw his growing up as a chronicle of her own aging, and it frightened and infuriated her. I learned too late that she slapped him constantly and yanked his hair, and once I caught her prepared to flog him with a riding crop.''

The images sickened Celia, and she saw her disgust reflected in Cameron's eyes.

''That's why I hated her,'' he said. ''But did I hate her enough to kill her? I honestly don't know.''

''Even if you did, could you have killed Randolph?''

A tortured cry escaped his lips. ''Never! I loved him more than life itself.''

One heart-wrenching sob burst forth from him, then he gritted his teeth and set his jaw and cried no more. When he turned to face her again, his eyes were dry and his expression inscrutable.

''I beg your forgiveness, Celia, for not telling you. When I realized how much I loved you, I tried to take you away from here, from me, to spare you this.''

''I wanted to stay. It wasn't all your doing.''

He stood, lifted her to her feet, and tilted her chin so that his gaze locked with hers. ''Can you still love me, knowing what I've told you?''

Part of her wanted to throw her arms around him and press her lips to his, to proclaim that she would love him forever, as she had promised when she married him. But another more prudent part held her back.

''I want to love you,'' she said, ''but I'm too confused. You must give me time to think, to sort all this out.''

He groaned and bent to kiss her, but she pushed away.

''And you must give me space to think as well,'' she added.

The color drained from his face and all expression with it. The look he gave her was a handsome mask, but whether it covered anger or pain, she couldn't tell.

''I'll give you time and space. If I have alienated you, it's my own fault.'' He pivoted and stalked back to the house, his back straight and proud.

What have you gotten yourself into now, Celia Stevens, she asked herself. And when she remembered her name was no longer Stevens but Alexander, she wept.

AS THE NOVEMBER DAYS shortened, Celia's confusion grew. The harder she tried to determine whether she believed Cameron was capable of murder, the more bewildered she became.

The night after he told her that he'd hated Clarissa, she moved from his room back into her own. She longed for his touch, but her doubts kept her from him. When she closed her eyes she was reminded of the bludgeoned bodies so graphically described by the newspapers and wondered if Cameron's gentle hands could have inflicted the injuries. After seeing her flinch and turn away a few times, Cameron withdrew into himself, breaking his habit of the past month when he would constantly grasp her hand, run his

fingers through her hair, or caress her cheek as if as-
suring himself that she really existed and wasn't a
figment of his imagination.

Cameron returned to the work of cataloging the
plants and animals of the prairies, swamps and salt
marshes, but he worked alone. Celia remained on the
island, sometimes helping Mrs. Givens, but mostly
wandering the beaches and trying to convince herself
beyond doubt that Cameron could not have killed his
family.

She had loved the mystery section of her Sand Castles bookstore and had devoured not only the classic
authors but also the contemporary favorites. She'd
learned much about motive and opportunity from her
reading, and she tried to apply that knowledge to the
problem before her.

The question of motive in the murders of Clarissa
and Randolph threw a major obstacle into her delib-
erations. Robbery hadn't been the goal, unless it was
botched in progress and the would-be thieves had fled
empty-handed. The only person to profit financially
from Clarissa's death was Cameron. If Clarissa's murder had been a crime of passion rather than greed,
Cameron again filled the bill. By his own admission,
he had hated Clarissa for her cruelty toward Randolph
and wished her dead.

In both instances, Randolph was the puzzle piece
that didn't fit. Neither of the motives demanded his
death—unless he had witnessed his mother being
killed and was silenced to protect the killer.

Opportunity also pointed the finger at Cameron.

He'd been in the house alone with his family with Mrs. Givens in Liverpool and the servants at the village festival—but such circumstances would have been ideal for an assassin outside the family as well.

And what about Cameron's own injuries? Had he been intended to die also, or had Clarissa inflicted those injuries in self-defense? The newspapers claimed the ineptitude of local investigators had contaminated the crime scene to the point where blood spatter patterns and other forensic evidence had proved worthless in assessing blame.

As the days passed, Celia wrestled with several possibilities. Cameron had killed his family in a drunken rage and had been too inebriated to remember. Robbers had attacked the family and been frightened away before stealing anything. But it was the third possibility that frightened Celia most of all, the possibility that she knew nothing of the true character of the man she'd married, that Cameron was a cold-blooded killer and a consummate actor who had planned and executed the murder of his wife and child to free himself of their presence in order to inherit Clarissa's fortune and retreat to his island paradise unencumbered by family responsibilities.

Her heart rejected every possibility but the second, but her pragmatism counseled caution, reminding her that only time would grant her a true assessment of the character of the man she had fallen so deeply in love with and thought she knew.

TWO WEEKS PASSED AFTER Celia had confronted Cameron with her knowledge of Clarissa and Randolph's murders, but she had found no answers and no peace. There could be none of either without the facts, and all the additional facts were either back in England or buried in Cameron's subconscious.

Or withheld from her purposely by him.

Accepting that the solution to the crime was beyond her reach, she was faced with a more immediate decision: whether to remain with Cameron on Solitaire until she regained her trust in him and, in doing so, absolve him of any blame, or flee to Key West and return to her home, turning her back on Cameron and Solitaire just as she had on Darren.

Her heart cried out against the latter. She hadn't loved Darren. She knew that now. Like a kindly older brother, the con man had offered her a way out of her lonely existence after the death of her parents. But she had bonded with Cameron in a love unlike any she had ever known. Did she give that love a chance to prove itself or flee for her life?

It was a choice she was reluctant to make, and fate was to take the decision out of her hands.

Chapter Twelve

"Have a piece of pie, m'dear. You're wasting away before my very eyes."

Mrs. Givens shoved the plate across the table toward Celia, but she shook her head. She'd had no appetite for weeks, and between eating very little and pacing the beaches, she'd lost enough pounds that her clothes hung loose.

Her routine on the island had reverted to the way it had been when she first arrived, with Cameron gone, often for days at a time, and Celia taking her meals with Mrs. Givens in the kitchen. The kindly old woman fussed over her, encouraging her to eat and trying to keep her mind occupied, but neither food nor busyness could mend what ailed Celia.

The chasm between her and Cameron grew wider each day. She had asked for time and space, but that space had grown into a gulf she feared neither of them would be able to cross again.

"Is there nothing I can do to make things better between the two of you?" Mrs. Givens asked. "I can see with my own eyes how miserable you both are. Can't you forget what's past and go on as before?''

"I wish it were that simple."

"Cameron's a good man. You must believe that." The housekeeper took Celia's untouched plate and scraped its contents into the scrap bucket for the compost heap.

Remembering mothers of serial killers whom she'd seen on television newscasts proclaiming the same thing, Celia smiled weakly at her. "How did Cameron treat Clarissa? Was he ever unkind to her?"

Mrs. Givens avoided Celia's gaze and busied herself with the washing up. "I don't know what you mean."

"Did he ever raise his voice? Hit her?"

"It wasn't what you think." The housekeeper threw her dishcloth into the soapy water and turned to face Celia. "He was protecting Randolph."

"From Clarissa?"

"Aye, from his own mother." Mrs. Givens's mouth puckered as if she'd tasted bitter fruit. "It was unnatural the way that woman treated the boy—and he was such a good boy, a dear little love."

"What did Cameron do to Clarissa?" Celia forced herself to ask, dreading the answer.

Mrs. Givens pushed back a gray curl with her wet hand. "At first he tried to reason with her, to understand why she mistreated the boy. When that didn't stop her tyranny, he yelled at her, but his threats didn't work either."

"So he hit her?"

Mrs. Givens flinched as if she'd been struck herself. "Just the one time. The day he caught her ready to beat Randolph with a riding crop. He snatched it from her hands and lashed out at her—but stopped himself before inflicting real harm. When he realized what he'd almost done, he was horrified."

"Did he hurt her?"

"Only her pride. Her clothing protected her from the glancing blow. But I believe his defense of Randolph made her hate the boy even more."

Celia felt sick to her stomach. "Did she continue to beat him when Cameron wasn't there?"

"Not that I know of. I don't think she ever touched the child after that."

"Are you implying Cameron knocked some sense into her?"

"No—" Mrs. Givens turned quickly back to her dishpan.

"Then what caused her change of heart?"

A long silence reigned in the room before the housekeeper answered. "She died."

Celia fled the kitchen. Cameron had told her Clarissa had whipped Randolph with a riding crop, but he hadn't mentioned he'd caught her at it right before she died. Had her abuse of their son sent Cameron over the edge, provoking him to murder?

But how could that explain Randolph's death?

She ran north along the beach, as far from the house as she could move and still remain on the island. The exertion of running and the heat of the midday sun warmed her uncomfortably, so she stripped off her clothes, tossed them in a heap on the sand, and plunged into the cool water.

The exercise helped ease the agitation in her mind, and she swam far out into the gulf. She stopped to rest, treading water, and gazed back at her enchanted island, her heaven turned hell. Her attention was drawn to a long, sleek cigarette boat headed for the island's northern point. As she watched, the boat glided toward shore, and its only occupant secured the anchor, climbed overboard, and waded ashore. He walked straight toward the dune where Celia had left her clothes.

She couldn't retrieve her clothing without being seen, and she had no idea what the man wanted on the island, whether he was a harmless recreational sailor or one of the dreaded drug-runners Mrs. Givens had warned her of.

Celia struck out toward the south, swimming parallel to the beach until she could no longer see the man among the dunes. Then she headed straight for shore, heedless of her nakedness as she raced through the surf, across the beach, and onto the path between the dunes.

She ran into the hallway, grabbed the conch shell Cameron had given her, and hurried out onto the east veranda. She'd no sooner finished the third trumpeting note when Mrs. Givens rushed in from the kitchen.

She took one look at Celia's nude form and stripped the pinafore from her dress. "Cover yourself, m'dear, and tell me what's the matter."

"There's a stranger on the north beach." She slipped the pinafore over her shoulders, crossed the sashes behind her back, and tied them in front. The width of the housekeeper's apron spanned her entire body, covering her front and back.

The thunder of running feet hit the veranda steps, and Noah burst into view.

"I was fixing that rotten board on the dock when I heard your signal." He wiped his sweaty face on his sleeve. "What's wrong?"

"A stranger on the island," Mrs. Givens said. "Get Mr. Alexander's gun—"

"That won't be necessary," a strange voice announced, its British accent coarser than Cameron's.

Celia turned toward a tall, angular man standing in the doorway to the dogtrot. He held an ominous semi-automatic pistol in one hand.

In the other were her clothes.

His black eyes flicked over Mrs. Givens and Noah, then raked over Celia, and a grin lit the small, dark eyes of his narrow face. "These must be yours."

The stranger held out Celia's clothes, but when she reached to take them, he jerked them back and pointed the pistol at her in a threatening gesture.

"Stay where you are—and as you are. I find your unusual attire quite—provocative." He threw back his head and laughed, exposing yellowed teeth.

"What do you want?" Mrs. Givens looked ready to do battle with the intruder.

Celia placed a restraining hand on the housekeeper's arm. The man appeared prepared to shoot. And enjoy it.

"All in good time, madam. All in good time." His speech and accent revealed some education, but his clothes were dirty and disheveled.

"Get in there and take a seat." The stranger waved the pistol at them and herded them before him into the dining room.

Mrs. Givens balked, but Celia nudged her forward, hoping that by cooperating they could stay alive until Cameron returned to rescue them. Celia wondered if Cameron had heard her signal or if he was too far away, planning to remain overnight on the mangrove islands as he'd done frequently the past two weeks. She shivered at the possibility of Cameron stumbling in on their unexpected visitor unawares, and the man before them shooting him from ambush.

"Sit," the stranger ordered, but when Celia tried to take a chair, he yelled at her. "Not you. Just those two. You get those ropes and tie them up."

While Celia retrieved the braided cords that held back the draperies, the stranger ordered Mrs. Givens and Noah to place their hands behind their backs. Then he instructed Celia to tie them fast.

"No need to gag you, I suppose," he said. "You the only ones on this island?"

"There's—" Mrs. Givens began, but Celia cut her off.

"I'm Mrs. Alexander. I'm a widow, and this is Mrs. Givens, my housekeeper, and our handyman, Noah. We're the only ones here."

A strange expression crossed his face, but the intruder simply shrugged. "Good. That makes things much easier."

"Who are you?" Celia asked, "and what do you want?"

"Better you don't know my name—but then I don't suppose it will matter, in the end. I'm Jack Utley."

Celia shuddered. If he revealed his identity, he was probably planning to kill them. "If it's money or supplies you want, take what you need and leave us in peace."

"I'll take all that, but I want more. Come with me, Mrs. Alexander." He motioned her into the hall with his pistol and pointed toward the stairs. "I want to see the rest of the house."

Celia doubted the house itself interested him. More likely, he was searching for anyone who might be hiding, or even worse, he planned to rape her once they were out of sight of the others. With his pistol jammed into the small of her back, she had no choice but to precede him up the steps.

Utley ordered her to open the door to each room and enter before he followed her inside. Her heart stopped when she entered Cameron's room and Utley opened the armoire to find Cameron's clothes arrayed there.

"I thought you said you were a widow," he said in a mocking tone.

"My husband died just a few weeks ago from encephalitis, and I've kept the room just as he left it."

Utley smiled with a warmth that didn't reach his eyes, then left the room. He immediately entered Celia's bedroom and focused on the wide bed with its rattan headboard and linen coverlet. Then his gaze traveled over Celia, and she wished for something less revealing than Mrs. Givens's apron, knowing the thin cotton fabric concealed very little, especially with the setting sun shining behind her.

Trying to keep her nervousness from showing, Celia went to her closet, took out her wedding shoes, and slipped them on. Utley watched her, his tongue flicking over his lips like a reptile's, and she could read the blatant lust on his ugly face.

She decided the best defense was a good offense and refused to cower before the man. "Why are you interested in my house, Mr. Utley?"

"Business, ma'am. A very profitable business." He crossed to the veranda and gazed out over the water, his carnal appetites seemingly forgotten.

"What business is there here in the middle of nowhere?"

"I have a delivery to make. A surprise for your husband."

"I told you. My husband's dead."

Utley laughed and shook his head. "Then there's a dead man sailing the boat that usually ties up at your dock. When do you expect him back?"

She wouldn't acknowledge that she'd lied. "What's your surprise?"

He glanced at the pistol he still held at the ready, but said nothing.

Celia, still uncomfortably aware of her state of undress, reached for the wrapper in her closet, but Utley leveled the pistol at her and shook his head.

"When do you expect Alexander back?" he repeated.

"I don't," she replied honestly. Unless Cameron had heard her conch call for help, he could stay away for days.

"No matter," Utley said. "I've been searching for him for over six years. A few hours, or even days, more or less, won't really matter. As long as I make my 'delivery'—" he pointed the gun and pretended to pull the trigger "—that's all that matters."

With a chilling certainty and growing fear, Celia realized that Utley had come to kill Cameron. And probably all the rest of them as well. She had to find a way to keep the man from shooting her, Mrs. Givens and Noah until Cameron could arrive and save them, or until Celia could think of a plan to overcome their visitor. An idea struck her, and she hurried to act.

"I've been an inconsiderate hostess. You must be thirsty and hungry after so many hours on the water. If you'll come down to the kitchen, I'll fix you something to eat." She raised the hem of the pinafore provocatively, allowing Utley a glimpse of her thigh. "After dinner," she said with what she hoped seemed like enthusiasm, "I'll see that your other…needs are taken care of."

Without waiting for an answer, Celia swept past

Utley into the hall. She held her breath and waited for a bullet in the back that never came.

He clattered down the stairs behind her, and she strode into the front room and selected the largest brandy snifter from the sideboard. After filling it almost to the brim, she handed it to Utley, who stood in the doorway, appearing slightly stunned by her behavior.

"Would you care to relax while I prepare your dinner, or would you rather come with me?" Celia flashed what she hoped was a come-hither smile and wiggled her hips as she brushed past him in the doorway.

Utley bolted down half the brandy and wiped his mouth on his sleeve. He grabbed her wrist as she attempted to pass, digging his fingernails into her flesh. "You're a smart one, Mrs. Alexander, and I don't trust you."

For a moment she feared he would shoot her on the spot, but he glanced at his half-empty glass, retrieved the brandy decanter, and waved his pistol at her again. "To the kitchen. I'm starving."

She avoided looking at Mrs. Givens and Noah as she passed the open doors of the dining room. They must have thought she'd gone mad, but there was method in her madness.

When Celia and Utley entered the kitchen, she pretended the pistol aimed at her head didn't exist. "Please have a seat, and I'll serve you."

An aromatic fish chowder Mrs. Givens had prepared for dinner bubbled on the stove, but it lacked an essential ingredient. Celia went to the shelf where Mrs. Givens stored her herbal remedies and took down the bottle that held the sleeping potion the housekeeper had once given her. After spooning up a bowl of chowder, Celia uncorked the bottle and poured a generous measure into the stew, hoping the onions and peppers would cover its bitter taste.

"What's that you're adding?" Utley's slurred words reflected both his suspicions and the progress of his drunkenness.

Celia placed the bowl in front of him and, repressing a shudder, rubbed her breast against his sleeve. "It's—oil of oysters, an aphrodisiac. I thought you might want such inspiration for later."

She batted her eyelashes at him suggestively and turned to cut bread from the loaf. She hefted the bread knife, wondering if she had the strength and the stomach to plunge it into his black heart, but he stopped her by pointing the pistol at her head again.

Abandoning the knife, she served him bread and butter, then sat across from him, filling and refilling the snifter as he ate. He finished off the first bowl of stew and demanded another. His speech became more slurred, but he showed no signs of passing out.

As he came closer to finishing his meal, his glances and comments became more suggestive, and Celia began to worry that she'd backed herself into a terrible trap.

"Would you like dessert?" she asked. "Mrs. Givens has made a wonderful bread pudding with lemon sauce."

The man pushed himself away from the table and stood, wobbling only slightly. A repulsive leer split his face. "I want only one thing for dessert."

With lightning speed and dexterity for someone who was supposed to be both drugged and drunk, he whipped out a hand and grabbed her. Wrapping his fingers in her hair, he pulled her face toward his, while his other hand held the pistol pointed at her heart.

"We're going to have a very long and busy night, pretty lady," he said with a hideous laugh.

His lips closed on Celia's. Despite her revulsion, she sensed a sudden movement on the veranda behind him. Someone jerked him away from her, and at the same instant, his pistol fired.

A searing pain burned Celia's chest, blackness closed around her, and she slumped to the floor.

Chapter Thirteen

Celia opened her eyes but couldn't move. Footsteps approached, and Mrs. Givens's sensible shoes appeared beside her. Either she and Noah had broken free or someone had untied them.

"God in heaven, are they both dead?" the housekeeper cried.

Strong arms lifted Celia to her feet. She smelled the sunshine and salt air on Cameron's clothes and buried her face in his throat, forgetting for the moment Clarissa and Randolph and the doubts she'd had, reveling in the warmth and security of his embrace.

Until Mrs. Givens gasped.

When Celia saw the pinafore soaked with blood, her legs buckled, and she'd have fallen if Cameron hadn't held her fast and eased her into a chair beside the stove. He scanned her with worried eyes while Mrs. Givens peeled back the edges of the pinafore over Celia's heart where the bullet had ripped through the fabric.

"Am I shot?" Celia asked, all too aware of the burning pain in her chest.

"The bullet cut a furrow like a corn row in you," Mrs. Givens said, "but it was only a glancing blow."

"I came as quickly as I could when I heard your signal," Cameron said, "but the tide and winds were against me."

While Cameron clasped Celia's hand, Mrs. Givens mopped her chest with cold water and cleansed away the blood. Then she smeared the wound with a sweet-smelling salve and bound it with clean linen.

Celia glanced at Cameron, whose jaw was set in a hard line and whose face flushed with fury as he glared at the prostrate form of Jack Utley on the kitchen floor.

"Is he dead?" Celia asked.

Noah approached the intruder and felt for a pulse. "The blood must be yours, Miss Celia, cause he ain't shot anywheres. But he's got a powerful bruise on his cheek where Mr. Alex hit him."

"Tie him up, Noah," Cameron ordered in a tone so cold that Celia shivered to hear it.

Noah disappeared, but returned immediately with the drapery cords and bound Utley hand and foot. "He ain't going nowheres anytime soon."

Mrs. Givens had also left the room and returned with Celia's robe. She held it up like a screen while Celia removed the bloody apron, then slipped it over Celia's arms and belted it around her. Celia slid weakly back into her chair.

"Who is he?" Cameron demanded in the same chilly voice.

"Jack Utley," Celia said. "He said he'd come to make a delivery, but I think he planned to kill you."

The housekeeper surveyed her kitchen, strewn with dirty dishes and pots, and caught sight of the empty bottle of herbal remedy. "Did you feed him all of that?"

Celia nodded. "I kept adding it to his food, but it seemed to have no effect."

"No effect?" She snorted with contempt. "You may as well bury him now, Noah. The devil will never wake up."

In contradiction to her words, Utley gave a low groan and fluttered his eyelids.

"You want me to hit him again?" Noah asked.

A look of black rage suffused Cameron's features. "I'll take care of him."

"Will you?" Celia asked.

He caught the irony in her words, and his tension eased, but only slightly. "Take him to the cowshed, Noah."

Cameron sat on the arm of Celia's chair and draped his arm around her. "Tell me what happened."

Celia related how she'd seen Utley's boat arrive at the north point, how he'd surprised them before they could arm themselves, of his intent to harm Cameron, and finally, how she'd beguiled the intruder into eating, then laced his food with Mrs. Givens's remedy.

Cameron's jaw tightened as Celia described Utley's advances, but he made no more threats against the man.

"What are you going to do with him?" Celia

asked. "We can't leave him tied in the cowshed forever."

"He'd sour the milk," Mrs. Givens said, and Celia realized the woman wasn't joking.

"We can't allow him to leave," Cameron said. "He might sneak back in the night and murder us all. That seems to have been his intention."

"Then you have no choice but to kill him," Celia taunted. She played a dangerous game with Utley's life in her effort to prove whether Cameron was capable of murder.

He studied her through narrowed eyes. "You may be right."

He stood abruptly, grabbed his rifle from where he'd propped it against the kitchen door, and headed toward the outbuildings.

Celia watched him go with a breaking heart.

"He can't just shoot the man," Mrs. Givens said. "You must stop him!"

"Cameron must do what he has to do. I will not be his conscience." Celia had set Cameron a test, and if he failed it, Utley would die. She wondered what kind of monster she'd become as she sat, listening for the sound of gunshots. Several minutes passed as she waited beneath Mrs. Givens's disapproving glare, and her resolve weakened and self-disgust filled her. She couldn't prove her husband's guilt or innocence at the expense of another man's life.

She rushed from the kitchen out into the yard and ran straight into Cameron as he returned from the cowshed. "Is he—"

"Sleeping like a baby and snoring so loudly the cow will have no rest tonight."

Relief flooded through her, but it didn't wash away the guilt she felt at pushing Cameron toward murder. "What are you going to do with him?"

"I must talk with you, Celia." He took her hand and walked with her into the house to the front parlor. "Sit down."

After propping his rifle against the wall, he moved to the fireplace, reached up and removed the portrait of Clarissa and Randolph. As Celia watched, puzzled and horrified, he slipped the knife he used for gutting fish from the sheath at his belt and attacked the painting.

"Don't!" she cried.

He paused, knife in midair, and she shivered at the tableau before her. Her protests proved futile, for he plunged the knife into the canvas once more and ripped it down its length. When he stopped, the painting hung in shreds with only one large chunk of it intact, the portion that held the smiling image of young Randolph.

Cameron lit the wood lying ready in the fireplace and fed the strips of canvas into the flames, all except the part that bore his son's picture, which he set carefully aside. He shattered the gilded frame into pieces over his knee and fed those, too, into the blazing fire.

When the flames burned low, he sat beside her and took her hands in his. "We must put the past behind us, Celia. Can you do that?"

She pulled her hands away. "You're asking too much of me."

"Am I? Do you believe we can live the rest of our lives as we have these past weeks, avoiding each other, yearning for the love we once had, hearing each other's movements behind the wall that separates our rooms, yet unable to breach the wall that divides our hearts?"

His eyes shone in the firelight, and she was shocked by the gauntness of his face. Cameron had lost even more weight than she had, and the unbearable burden of their estrangement weighed heavily on them both.

"You can try for another week," he said, "another year, and another, but you will not solve the mystery of who killed my family. God knows, I have tried for almost eight years, and I still have no answers."

She buried her face in her hands to block the sight of his tortured face. "I don't know—"

"You must choose. Tomorrow morning, you and I and Utley will sail for Key West."

His announcement caught her by surprise. "You never leave Solitaire."

"We can't set Utley free to threaten us again, and, in spite of what you think of me, I can't kill him. I must take him to the authorities and let them deal with him. After all, the man attempted to kill you."

Celia wanted to trust Cameron, to love him as unconditionally as she had when she married him, but the strange circumstances of the deaths of Clarissa and Randolph had planted too many suspicions in her mind.

"Why do *I* have to go with you?" she asked.

His eyes burned with amber fire. "When we reach Key West, you must make your decision."

"About what?"

"You have two choices. You can choose to become my legally wedded wife."

"And my second choice?" She returned his fiery gaze, but this time he refused to meet her eyes.

"I will destroy the document that certifies our marriage and arrange for your transportation home. Our marriage will be null and void, as if it never happened."

"I don't know if I could choose either of those now," she admitted honestly.

Cameron grasped her by the shoulders, and she feared for a moment that he would shake her, but his hands eased their grip and his fingers traveled upward, caressing her throat and face before he released her.

"You have until we reach Key West to make up your mind. Whichever you choose has to be better than the hell we've existed in these past weeks. We'll sail at dawn."

She heard him leave the room and climb the stairs, but she remained, struggling with the dilemma before her and watching the last fragments of Clarissa's portrait disintegrate into ashes.

MRS. GIVENS SHOOK Celia awake in the predawn darkness, and she opened her eyes reluctantly. She had lain awake for hours after going to bed, listening to Cameron tossing and turning in the next room and trying to decide what she would do once they reached Key West.

"Mr. Alexander told me to pack all your things," the housekeeper said with a questioning look and held up a piece of fine leather luggage. "I found this in the attic."

While Celia hurriedly washed and dressed, Mrs. Givens took her clothes from the dresser and armoire and placed them in the suitcase. "That's everything. Except your seashells."

Celia considered the collection of shells in their basket on the table by her bed. If she decided to leave Solitaire for good, she'd at least have them to remember. "I'll carry those myself."

Mrs. Givens waited for a moment, as if hoping Celia would give some explanation, but since she had no idea what her ultimate decision would be, Celia couldn't explain what was happening. The housekeeper, recognizing that she'd get no answers about the strange events of the morning, left the room, muttering under her breath.

Celia pulled on her sneakers and tied them tightly. Even had the bloodstains not ruined them, her wedding slippers would have been too treacherous on the deck of the sailboat.

Mrs. Givens reappeared, bearing a tray filled with fruit, hot biscuits and a steaming cup of coffee, and set it on the table beside Celia.

She drank the coffee gratefully, hoping it would clear the cobwebs from her mind, but the food stuck in her throat, and she could only manage a few bites.

The housekeeper, twisting her apron in her hands, stood watching her. When Celia finished her coffee and set the cup aside, Mrs. Givens spoke.

"You must beg Mr. Alexander not to make this trip." A note of hysteria tinged her voice.

"Are you afraid of what might happen if the authorities discover who he is?" Celia asked.

She knew that Scotland Yard had released Cameron for lack of evidence, but she also knew that he feared the police might appear at any time with additional facts or a surprise witness to incriminate him.

"I've had another premonition," Mrs. Givens said, "unlike any I've ever had before." Her eyes filled with tears, and her skin appeared gray in the lamplight.

Celia shook her head. "Neither your premonitions nor any pleas of mine will change Cameron's mind about going to Key West."

"But this vision is different." The housekeeper's voice was almost a whisper. "I see it as clear as I see the nose on your face. I *know* what's going to happen to you."

Celia scoffed at the woman's eerie pronouncement. "How can you know the future, when I haven't decided myself what I'm going to do?"

"I only know, m'dear, that if you leave this place today, you are going somewhere far, far away, and I fear I may never see you again." She buried her face in her apron and sobbed. "And I love you like my own daughter, I do."

"Please don't cry." Celia hugged the housekeeper

and fought back her own tears. She'd come to love
Mrs. Givens, and the thought of never seeing her
again saddened Celia deeply.

On impulse, Celia removed the diamond studs from
her ears, the earrings she had worn since the disastrous day she'd almost married Darren, and pressed
them into Mrs. Givens's hands. "These are for you."

"I can't, not your diamonds."

"I want you to have them, to remember me by if
I don't return, and to remember how dear you are to
me, whether I come back to Solitaire or not."

Mrs. Givens dried her eyes. "Take care of Cameron, m'dear."

Celia thought her parting words strange, but Cameron was calling from the foot of the stairs, so she
kissed the housekeeper's wrinkled cheek, picked up
the leather bag, and hurried down to meet him.

He had gone on to the dock, and she found him
there with Noah. Noah and Cameron had already
lifted Utley, his hands and feet still bound, into the
bow of the boat, where he slumped groggily against
the seat. Cameron climbed into the stern, stowed her
bag and lifted her down beside him.

"Goodbye, Miss Celia," Noah said. "I'm gonna
miss you."

Both Noah and Mrs. Givens acted as if she
wouldn't be returning, and Celia wondered if that was
what Cameron had told them. As the boat slipped
away from the dock, she watched Noah, waving in
the weak light of dawn, until they rounded the southern tip of the island and she could see him no more.

Cameron headed the boat westward into deep water before turning south, and Celia glanced back to see dawn break over Solitaire. The eastern sky, striated with gold and lavender, illuminated the weathered gray boards of the graceful house and the profusion of magenta bougainvillea with pearly light, while the rising sun tinged the sand and azure gulf with pink. Through the swirling mists, she could spot the tiny form of Mrs. Givens, watching their departure from the upper veranda, and her heart swelled with love for the island, the house and its inhabitants.

Celia didn't want to contemplate never returning there.

Cameron sat beside her at the tiller, and as the sun rose higher and the first rays struck his profile, she saw in him the kind and exciting man she'd married, not the haggard worried Cameron of the past few weeks. He was risking discovery of his well-protected hiding place after over six years of seclusion, just to bring a worthless criminal to justice. Was that the behavior of a killer?

Cameron turned and caught her staring. ''Have you made your choice?''

Celia could read the fear in his eyes and knew he dreaded her decision, expecting the worst.

''Not yet,'' she said.

''We'll reach Key West before tonight. You can't delay much longer.''

They sailed in silence for hours with Utley only semiconscious in the bow. All the while, Celia turned the facts of her dilemma over and over in her mind.

Cameron had been right the night before when he'd insisted all the time in the world would not solve the enigma of the deaths of Clarissa and Randolph, but as Celia watched her husband at the tiller with the wind in his hair and the sun bronzing his skin, she accepted another fact that time would never change.

"Cameron," she called to him above the wind.

He turned to her with an anxious look. "You've decided?"

She shook her head. "I wanted to tell you that no matter what I decide, I will always love you."

Without releasing the tiller, he reached with his free arm and pulled her to him, crushing his lips to hers. She abandoned all thought of the future and reveled in the rightness of his embrace. She knew then that she could never leave Cameron, that the man she loved was no killer, and the life they shared on Solitaire meant more to her than any questions about Clarissa's murder. She was prepared to tell him her choice when a croaking voice interrupted.

"Water," Utley begged. "Please, water."

"What did you mean about waiting six years to kill Cameron?" Celia demanded.

Utley refused to answer. After a moment, he begged for water again.

Remembering how Mrs. Givens's remedy had made her mouth feel like cotton, Celia took pity on the man. She crawled to the back of the boat and held a bottle of water while he drank greedily.

"Not too much at once," she warned. "It could make you sick."

"The only thing that makes me sick," Utley said with a leering grin, "is that our plans for last night were interrupted—what with your *late* husband rising miraculously from the dead."

He looked toward Cameron, taunting him, and Celia wondered why a bound man would provoke someone to pound the daylights out of him.

"You must find a great deal of pleasure," Utley continued, "between those long, brown legs. You're a lucky man. You wouldn't want to share that bounty with me now, would you?" He licked his lips.

Cameron ignored him and kept his eye on the sails and sea, even though the calm of the water and the clear sky required little attention. In the light, persistent wind, the boat could have almost sailed itself.

"Why don't we settle this thing man to man?" Utley asked an hour later. "No need to bring in the law. We could fight it out here and now, and the winner gets the woman and the island."

"Why should I fight you for what is rightfully mine?" Cameron asked, unperturbed. "Especially when you're in no position to take it from me."

"Maybe because you're a betting man?"

Celia saw Utley's purpose clearly now. He had no chance of escape bound as he was, but if he could incite Cameron's anger, and have Cameron untie him to fight, he might prevail.

"You mustn't anger my husband," Celia told him. "You're tied up and helpless to defend yourself. If you make him angry, he could beat you senseless or shoot you, and you couldn't raise a finger to protect yourself.''

''Not him,'' Utley said in a voice that dripped with sarcasm. ''I know a gentleman when I see one, all high-minded and moral. He'd never strike anyone who couldn't strike back.''

Utley was right. He'd seen instantly what had been staring Celia in the face for the past few weeks, and she'd failed to see. Cameron's innate goodness shone through like a beacon. Such a man was incapable of murder. She started to speak, to beg Cameron's forgiveness for doubting him, to tell him that she wanted to make their marriage legally binding, but a glance ahead made her forget her words.

''Cameron, look,'' she shouted.

''Damn,'' Utley cried. ''We're heading straight into a squall.''

A blast of wind hit the sails, almost overturning the boat. Celia felt her pulse increase and her chest tighten. She forced herself to breathe slowly and deeply in hope of fighting off a panic attack.

''Cut me loose,'' Utley cried. ''I'll drown if we capsize.''

The high wind held, tossing the boat like a cork on the seas, and the gentle waves swelled into monstrous mountains.

Cameron reefed the sails, then fought the tiller with both hands while the wind ripped the sheets, and the boat crashed down into a valley between the waves.

''Cut me loose. I can help!'' Utley cried.

Without waiting for Cameron's approval, Celia

yanked his knife from its sheath, clambered across the heaving deck, and sawed at Utley's bonds.

"Hurry up, woman!" Utley had to yell into her ear to be heard above the wind.

When the last strand of rope fell away, he rubbed his wrists, then rushed to trim the sails even more. Celia huddled in the stern, holding on for dear life.

Once she caught Cameron's glance, a burning look of love and anxiety, before he returned his full attention to keeping the boat afloat.

"Strike the sail," Cameron screamed to Utley. "It's our only chance."

Suddenly, as if a giant hand had swatted the boat from the water, it rose into the air, hung for a moment on the force of the gale, then plummeted into the sea.

Chapter Fourteen

The boat crashed onto the surface of the water, and only Cameron's arm around her waist kept Celia from pitching overboard.

Utley, however, wasn't so lucky. An immense wave knocked him off the deck and into the sea.

Cameron didn't hesitate. After transferring the tiller to Celia, he dived into the roiling waters after their prisoner.

"Cameron, come back!" Celia screamed into the wind. "He's not worth risking your life for."

Sheets of heavy rain obscured her view, and she strained for a glimpse of Cameron in the storm-tossed sea. How could she have doubted him? He had placed his own life in jeopardy to save a man who'd intended to kill them both. And if Cameron drowned in the rescue attempt, he would never know her decision to trust him completely, to love him unconditionally.

She held on to the tiller with all her strength and prayed as she'd never prayed in her life.

The sky lightened around her as the squall line

passed, but even in the better light, she could spot no sign of Cameron or Utley on the calming water.

Suddenly, a splash sounded on the starboard side, and she turned as Cameron was levering himself into the boat.

"Utley?" she asked.

"I've got him. Help me pull him on board."

Fighting against the man's deadweight, Celia helped Cameron tug Utley over the side and onto the deck.

"Is he drowned?" she asked.

Cameron pressed his fingers to the man's neck. "He has a pulse. He's probably unconscious from the blow he took to the head when he pitched into the sea." He pointed to a bruised knot on Utley's temple. "Strip off his wet clothes and wrap him in blankets. I want this sorry excuse for a human being alive when we reach Key West."

Celia shivered at the violence in Cameron's tone and the fury in his eyes. Would she ever understand the contradictions in this man she loved more than life itself? One minute he was risking his life to save a criminal, and the next he looked as if he'd take great pleasure in feeding the very same man to the sharks.

Cameron took the tiller again, and Celia scurried to find dry blankets. She longed to tell Cameron of her decision to put the past behind her and to stay with him on Solitaire, but the cold anger in his eyes and the unyielding set of his mouth rebuffed her. Instead, she maintained a silent vigil over the unsavory man sprawled on the deck.

Hours later, when they entered the marina at Key West, Utley had yet to regain consciousness.

Cameron secured the boat and climbed onto the dock. "I'll have the harbormaster call the police."

Celia watched him stride down the wooden planks toward the marina office, his back stiff, his steps angry. He seemed so distant, so incensed, that she began to wonder whether, once she told him she wanted to stay on Solitaire, he would allow her to return.

CAMERON HASTENED HIS pace as he neared the quaint bed-and-breakfast where, eight hours ago a Key West police officer had taken Celia. The architecture of the structure reminded him of his house on the island, but he felt no pang of homesickness. Only an urgency to hold Celia in his arms.

He picked up his key at the front desk and hurried up the stairs to their room overlooking the tropical gardens at the back of the building. Not wanting to awaken Celia, he eased the door open slowly. His heart swelled with tenderness when he saw her lying asleep among the pillows, the duvet thrown back to reveal the magnificence of her long legs threaded through the sheets.

He'd last seen her at the police station. She'd thrown him a panicked look when the officer led her away after a brief interview. Cameron had wanted to assure her everything would be all right, but the detectives who'd been interrogating him pulled him back into the interview room before he could speak with her.

Lowering himself to the edge of the bed, he brushed back the golden strands of hair from her forehead. Immediately her eyes flew open, and she struggled upright.

"Where have you been?" Anxiety mixed with drowsiness in her husky voice. "I thought they'd arrested you."

Cameron shook his head. "The police had a great many questions."

As much as he longed to tell her, he restrained himself from pouring out the whole story. First, he wanted to hear her decision, to learn whether or not she had decided to trust him, to love him, to remain his wife. He had never known true happiness until Celia had set foot on his island, had never realized a man could love a woman so completely and unreservedly. But if they were to make a life together, he had to believe that Celia felt the same.

Fearful of her answer, but needing to know, he grasped her gently by the shoulders, then tilted her chin until their gazes met. "Have you decided?"

She lifted her arms and twined them around his neck. Her lips curved in a smile that turned his insides to jelly. "I decided long before we reached Key West, but you seemed so angry, I was reluctant to tell you."

His heart sank. "Because you feared your decision would make me more angry?"

She shook her head, her expression solemn. "I was afraid you'd say you didn't want me, even though I'd decided to stay."

With a groan he crushed her in his arms. "Not want you? My God, Celia, I'd sooner not want to breathe."

She snuggled against his chest and nuzzled against his throat. "Does that mean you'll take me back to Solitaire with you?"

He cupped her face in his hands. "Wherever I am, you will be there, or my life will be over."

With a sigh of pleasure, she lifted her lips to his. "I love you, Cameron. Without reservation, without doubt. I trust you with my heart and my life."

He returned her kiss with tears welling in his eyes. She trusted him, she loved him, not knowing the truth.

It was time to tell her.

"I had good reason to be angry yesterday. When Utley was taunting me, my memories of the night Clarissa and Randolph died suddenly returned. I had seen Jack Utley before."

Celia grew still. "I'm listening."

"He's the man who murdered my wife and child, who almost killed me, too. It was Utley I remembered striking with my fist, but I was too drunk to be a match for him."

"Did you tell this to the police?"

He drew her into the circle of his arm and leaned against the headboard. "That's why I was gone so long. They've been burning up the telephone lines all night with calls and faxes to Scotland Yard."

Her beautiful face glowed with happiness. "Then your name is cleared?"

"Better still, my conscience is clean. Unidentified

fingerprints at the crime scene have now been recognized as Utley's.''

''Then you can go home. To London? To Devon?''

''*We* can go home.'' He studied her face, anxious for any sign of hesitation.

''Home, my darling, is wherever you are.'' A sudden frown clouded her features, and his heart clenched with nervousness as he feared she might be having second thoughts.

''What was Utley's motive?'' she asked.

Cameron relaxed and drew her closer into his arms. ''When Utley realized the police had an eyewitness and fingerprints to tie him to the crime, he told them everything. Seems my dear cousin Christopher coveted my fortune and had hired Utley to kill me and my family in order to inherit. But Utley botched the job and left me alive. He came after me to finish what he started and eliminate me as a potential witness to his crime.''

''Thank God he failed,'' Celia said with a fervor that warmed him.

''Scotland Yard already has my cousin in custody. He won't be receiving my inheritance since Utley didn't kill me.''

''Then there's nothing more to do here?''

''Most definitely. We have some very urgent business.''

She attempted to rise. ''Then I should get dressed.''

''That,'' Cameron assured her, ''would be counterproductive.''

She arched a delicate eyebrow. "What do you mean?"

"You've already proved this very comfortable bed is fit for sleeping. I suggest we put it to another test."

She came into his embrace like a blessing, and if a man could die of happiness, Cameron figured he wouldn't survive the day.

SIX MONTHS LATER ON A warm and sunny May afternoon, Celia stood gazing out to sea. The swells of the Atlantic and the red earth of the Devon hills were nothing like the tranquil Gulf of Mexico and the white sugar sand of Solitaire, but the vista pleased her nonetheless. She and Cameron had made the estate their home ever since their wedding in the chapel there on Christmas day. Cameron had hired a manager to run the mine offices and now spent his days, with Celia's assistance, writing his book on the flora and fauna of the Ten Thousand Islands.

When Tracey arrived in England in December for the wedding, she brought a video of a television news magazine that featured Gregory Conroy, alias Darren Walker, alias David Weller, and half a dozen other assumed names. The man had just been indicted for murder by a grand jury in Massachusetts. Not, ironically, for the murder of Mrs. Seffner's daughter, but of another woman, another of his many wives who had died mysterious deaths. This victim's brother was a Boston detective who hadn't rested until he tracked Conroy down and proved his guilt.

Tracey, aware of Celia's near brush with disaster

with Darren, at first had reservations about Cameron.
But the Englishman soon won her over with his
warmth and gentle kindness. Celia rewarded Tracey's
approval by nixing pink gowns for her attendants this
time and choosing instead deep green velvet for the
holiday season.

The wedding in the chapel decorated with holly,
ivy and red velvet bows, had been attended by hundreds of Cameron's friends, business associates and
even a sprinkling of royalty. He had been well-liked
before the tragic murders, and with his name cleared,
had been welcomed back to England with enthusiasm.
They had welcomed Celia, too.

Remembering, Celia smiled. In the months since
their wedding, her days with Cameron had been the
happiest she'd ever known. She hadn't even missed
Sand Castles, which she'd sold to Tracey after the
wedding. In anticipation of seeing her husband soon,
she turned back toward the house.

Mrs. Givens had left the tea tray on the terrace
where the soft breeze was heavy with the scent of
roses warmed by the sun, but Celia was waiting for
Cameron, who had taken an overseas call in his study.

Soon, however, Cameron strode through the French
doors, a smile creasing his handsome face. Her heart
jolted, as it did each time she saw him again after the
briefest of separations, with the knowledge of how
much she loved this kind and gentle man.

"Good news," he announced.

Celia moved to the tea table, took her seat and

poured her husband a cup. "The mines are doing well?"

Cameron took the cup and saucer, moved a chair closer to hers and sat beside her. "That, too. But this is even better news. It's about Noah."

"But we just had news of Noah a few weeks ago. Captain Biggins won't pick up mail at Solitaire for two more months."

Cameron sipped his tea, set his cup aside, and rubbed his hands with pleasure. "The news isn't from Noah. It's about Noah. Remember how Noah was hiding from the police because, ironically, like me, he'd been wrongly accused of murder?"

Celia nodded. "I've thought of him often over the past months, poor man, stranded all alone on Solitaire."

"He won't have to stay a moment longer if he doesn't want to. I've sent Captain Biggins to tell him."

"But he'll be arrested."

Cameron shook his head. "One of the men who accused Noah has been arrested for another crime. As part of a plea bargain, he's told the authorities the truth. The real murderer has been arrested, and Noah is free."

"That's wonderful news! Do you think he'll come here to live with us?"

"I've invited him. But he has money of his own and can go wherever he wishes."

Celia smiled, filled with happiness for her old friend and with the secret she was about to share with

Cameron. "It seems today's a day for good news. I have some of my own."

Cameron draped his arm around her shoulders and kissed her forehead. "You've found the roses you wanted to add to the garden?"

She shook her head. "But you're warm. My news does have to do with a nursery."

Cameron's gaze held such love and reverence it brought tears to her eyes. "A baby?"

"No."

He seemed to shrivel with disappointment, and she took instant pity on him. "Not one baby. Two. We're expecting twins."

Cameron whooped with joy, pushed back his chair with such force that it clattered on the terrace floor, and swept her into his arms. "Celia, you are marvelous!"

She laughed with delight. "Me? You deserve at least half the credit."

"You've made me the happiest man alive."

He twirled her around the terrace until the sea and the green Devon hills formed a kaleidoscope of colors and textures, broken only by the stout figure of Mrs. Givens in the doorway, wiping tears from her eyes with the corner of her apron.

* * * * *

Look for Charlotte Douglas's next title,

SURPRISE INHERITANCE,

in March 2003 from
Harlequin American Romance.

HARLEQUIN®
INTRIGUE®

Elevates breathtaking romantic suspense to a whole new level!

When all else fails, the most highly trained, covert agents are called in to "recover" the mission. This elite group is known as

THE SPECIALISTS

Nothing is too dangerous for them... except falling in love.

DEBRA WEBB

does it again with an explosive new trilogy for Harlequin Intrigue. You'll recognize some of the names from her popular COLBY AGENCY series, but hang on to your hats this time out. Because THE SPECIALISTS are more dangerous, more daring...and more deadly than any agents you've ever seen!

UNDERCOVER WIFE
January

HER HIDDEN TRUTH
February

GUARDIAN OF THE NIGHT
March

Look for them wherever Harlequin books are sold!

HARLEQUIN®
Makes any time special®

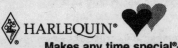

HARLEQUIN®
INTRIGUE®

Cupid has his bow loaded with double-barreled romantic suspense that will make your heart pound. So look for these **special Valentine selections** from Harlequin Intrigue to make your holiday breathless!

McQUEEN'S HEAT
BY HARPER ALLEN

SENTENCED TO WED
BY ADRIANNE LEE

CONFESSIONS OF THE HEART
BY AMANDA STEVENS

Available throughout January and February 2003 wherever Harlequin books are sold.

HARLEQUIN®
Makes any time special ®

For more on Harlequin Intrigue® books, visit www.tryintrigue.com   HIVAL